Books by Rebecca Brandewyne

Silhouette Nocturne

From the Mists of Wolf Creek #65

MIRA Books

Dust Devil
Glory Seekers
High Stakes
Destiny's Daughter
The Love Knot
The Ninefold Key
The Crystal Rose

REBECCA BRANDEWYNE

is a bestselling author of historical novels. Her stories consistently place on the bestseller lists, including those of the *New York Times* and *Publishers Weekly*. She was inducted into the *Romantic Times BOOKreviews* Hall of Fame in 1988, and is a recipient of the magazine's Career Achievement Award (1991). She has also received *Affaire de Coeur*'s Golden Quill Pen Award for Best Historical Romance, along with a Silver Pen Award.

REBECCA BRANDEWYNE

From the MISTS of WOLF CREEK

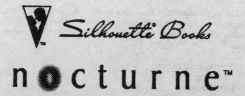

Silhouette Books

nocturne™

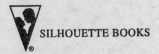

SILHOUETTE BOOKS

ISBN-13: 978-0-373-61812-5

Recycling programs for this product may not exist in your area.

FROM THE MISTS OF WOLF CREEK

www.silhouettenocturne.com

Printed in U.S.A.

Dear Reader,

"Where do you get your ideas?" That's invariably the question most asked of writers.

So, what does inspire a tale? In the case of *From the Mists of Wolf Creek*, the answer might surprise you—because it was actually my two dogs who gave me the idea for this particular novel. One of my dogs is a beautiful black long-haired German shepherd. He looks and acts very much like the wolf in my story. My other dog is a sassy Australian cattle dog (red heeler) mix. He reminds me of my book's hero, Trace—someone who drifted around quite a lot before finally finding a good home. My dogs are the best of pals, to the point that each somehow always knows what the other is thinking. They're both extremely loving and protective, also, offering exactly the kind of care I thought my heroine, Hallie, needed in this novel. So she got a wolf and a man, courtesy of my two dogs—and of her own grandmother, a woman wise in the ways of Magick who casts a powerful spell that enchants more than one heart at Meadowsweet Farm, on the banks of Wolf Creek.

Happy reading!

Rebecca Brandewyne
www.brandewyne.com

For Wulfie and Buddy,
who inspired this tale.
With all my love.

From the Mists of Wolf Creek

The wolf padded silently
From the mists of Wolf Creek
Into the magic circle
Where a wise witch did speak.
With her jeweled pewter wand,
She touched him on his head,
Cast a spell of enchantment
That bound him and so led
To his role as protector
At old Meadowsweet Farm.
There, he would forever stay,
Keeping all free from harm.

The man padded silently
From the mists of Wolf Creek
Into the magic circle
Where a wise witch did speak.
With her jeweled pewter wand,
She touched him on his chest,
Cast a spell of enchantment
That drew forth all his best,
Eased the pain of the past,
And bound him to the farm.
There, he would forever stay,
A stout heart, a strong arm.

When the spell was finally done,
Not the wolf nor the man
Knew where one of them ended
And the other began.
Sharing a deep and special bond,
They were as one, soul and mind,
Their dreams and their thoughts
Now and always entwined.
Laid upon them was this charge:
Guard the farm; keep it well;
And when love comes softly
To cast its magic spell...

Like the mists from Wolf Creek,
Greet it with willing arms
And with a faithful heart.
Revel in all its charms.
Both wolf and man listened hard
To the wise witch's song.
For too many full moons,
They'd wandered far and long.
But the mists from Wolf Creek,
Now sweetly both bespelled,
And love came as promised,
At Meadowsweet e'er dwelled.

Prologue

A Spell Is Cast

Meadowsweet Farm, Wolf Creek, The Present

Death drew ever closer.

With her heightened senses, always so keenly attuned to her surroundings and her own being, Henrietta Taylor had discerned its inexorably nearing presence for some time now.

At first it had only lurked in the shadows and hovered at the edges of her consciousness. She had caught only occasional glimpses of it then—

a fluttering of its amorphous cloak, an inscrutable glance from beneath its voluminous hood.

Sunlight and her sheer strength of will had held it at bay for a while.

But eventually over the passing months, Death had grown bolder and less patient.

Now, sometimes late at night when she lay sleeping, it slipped into her old Victorian farmhouse, into her bedroom, and sat upon her shallowly rising and falling chest, peering down impenetrably into her slumbering face, as though to steal away her last breath finally and forever.

No doubt, with these tactics, Death hoped to frighten her, as it did so many others.

But unlike them, Henrietta was not afraid. She had lived too long and seen too much for that. She knew Death was but the guide to another dimension, another plane of existence not yet fully understood by those who dwelled in the physical realm.

When she passed beyond the door through which Death would lead her, she would see her parents and Jotham and Rowan again, and she would be glad of that.

But before then, she must do everything in her power to protect those she would be leaving behind—especially her namesake and granddaughter, Hallie.

That was the reason for the ritual Henrietta was undertaking tonight and why she had gone to such great lengths to prepare for it.

For months, she had befriended the huge wild black wolf around which her ceremony would center, gradually gaining its trust and confidence. For weeks, she had gathered the herbs and other plants she intended to employ, neatly cutting them with her bone-handled boline, then drying and preparing them for grinding with her mortar and pestle. For days, she had consulted her almanacs and correspondence tables to ensure that her timing would prove auspicious and her tools appropriate to her spellwork. Earlier this evening she had bathed in the nearby creek in order to cleanse and purify herself, then carefully dressed in her best witching clothes and flowing cloak.

Now Henrietta was ready.

Above the sweet meadow in which she stood—and for which her farm had been named—the moon shone bright and full, a gleaming silver orb in the black-velvet night sky. From the creek that wound through the woods encompassing the meadow, wisps of mist drifted ghostily, enshrouding the gnarled old trees and blanketing the gentle hollows of the land.

With her black-handled, double-edged, singing arthame and the carefully knotted cingulum she took from around her waist, Henrietta began the casting of the magic circle she required for this night's work, marking the perimeter with small stones she had collected some days before and set to one side for just this purpose.

When she had finished, she approached the round wooden table she had set up as her altar. There, she took up a little bowl of finely ground sea salt and, walking *deiseil* or clockwise, scattered it along the circle's boundary, chanting as she did so. Next she lit a cone of incense in her thurible and waved the smoke from the ornate brass burner around the circumference, continuing to chant softly. Then she set a candle aflame, anointed it with oil and bore it clockwise along the ring's edge. Last but not least, she uncorked a small bottle of holy water and sprinkled that around the periphery, so the magic circle had been cleansed and consecrated with all four elements: earth, wind, fire and water.

After that, Henrietta ignited the bonfire she had laid earlier beneath the large iron cauldron that hung from a tripod she had placed at the heart of the meadow, inside the circle she had cast. Then she called the Quarters and welcomed the God and Goddess she had worshiped for many long years now.

Finally, taking a deep breath, she beckoned to the great wolf, which had been watching her curiously, intently, from the bank of the misted creek. As he loped toward her, she used her arthame to cut a metaphysical door into the circle for him to pass through, then closed it securely behind him.

No more than she feared Death did Henrietta fear the wolf. He was a creature of nature, and she had always shared a special affinity with those, frequently finding them far preferable to people. Indeed, the older she had grown, the less tolerant she had become of the latter, until, now, with the exception of a chosen few, she was virtually a recluse.

Still, Henrietta never felt a lack. Her life at the farm was rich and full in all the ways that mattered to her. She knew what was important—and what was not. It seemed to her that the world was an increasingly cruel, vicious place, of which she no longer wanted any part. For her, life began and ended at Meadowsweet—which was why it must be protected.

As the massive wolf prowled restlessly around the magic circle, Henrietta determinedly set to work, lighting several more candles and, with her mortar and pestle, grinding the herbs and other plants she needed for her powerful spell. She knew what she hoped to achieve this night would take every ounce of her strength, will and faith.

Still, in the end—the God and Goddess willing—she would succeed.

Once she had all the necessary ingredients together, Henrietta put them into the cauldron over the blazing bonfire. As the big kettle began to bubble and smoke, she rang the pewter bell that sat upon the altar. Then, with her left hand, she took up her bejeweled pewter wand and, with her right hand, drew her arthame from the cingulum now wrapped around her waist.

With the wand, she struck the arthame just so, making it sing—pure, sweet notes that echoed melodiously across the meadow into the swirling mist and caused the wolf's ears to prick forward attentively.

Then, starting once more to chant and summoning her vast power born of the blessed Earth Mother, Henrietta began to work her elaborate spell of enchantment, calling the immense wolf to her side and touching him lightly with her wand....

Chapter 1

The Storm and the Wolf

A Two-Lane Highway, The Present

There was a storm coming on.

Hallie Muldoon could see it ahead in the distance, where leaden thunderclouds seethed and roiled on the horizon, blotting out the westering sun. At the sight, the strange, nebulous sense of anxiety and urgency she had felt ever since learning of her grandmother's unexpected death last month heightened within her, and she pressed her foot even harder against the accelerator of the car she drove.

In response, the sporty red Mini Cooper S shot down the narrow two-lane highway that was a patchwork of macadam bounded on either side by long, sweeping green verges abloom with a profusion of wildflowers, beyond which lay checkerboard fields of ripening grain.

Under other circumstances, it would have been a picturesque scene. But at the moment, beneath the lowering sky, it was somehow reminiscent of Van Gogh's painting *Starry Night,* and Hallie suffered the disturbing sensation that she was journeying into the distorted realm of an unquiet mind instead of toward the small town of Wolf Creek, her childhood home.

She had not been there since her mother, Rowan Muldoon, had passed away and Gram had sent her back East to live with her two great-aunts, Gram's spinster sisters, Agatha and Edith. That had been many years ago now, and the beginning of an entirely new life for Hallie, the old one—the one she would have lived had her mother survived—having died along with the only parent she had ever known.

Hallie thought that in some respects, nothing had gone right in her life since that moment.

In sharp contrast to Meadowsweet, the quiet, relatively isolated farm where Gram had lived, Great-Aunts Agatha and Edith had resided in a crowded, noisy big city, in a dark old gloomy town house wherein the sunshine, freedom and laughter to which the then seven-year-old Hallie had been accustomed had been painfully taboo. In the great-aunts' town house, the long heavy curtains were always drawn against the sun that would otherwise have faded the furniture and carpets, and little girls were to obey the rules, the primary of which had been to be seen and not heard. Natural childhood curiosity and chatter had brought severe frowns and censure.

As a result, back East, Hallie had quickly learned to keep her mouth shut and her thoughts to herself, to slip like a wraith through the shadowy halls of the town house, and to apply herself diligently to her studies at the private school in which the great-aunts had enrolled her, rather than wasting her time with such frivolous pursuits as idle daydreaming and rowdy playing.

In adulthood and retrospect, Hallie had realized the great-aunts had no doubt loved her dearly and meant well. It was just that having no experience with children of their own, they had reared her in the same fashion that their austere, Bible-thumping father, the Reverend Bernard Dewhurst, had reared them, knowing no other way. In the end, they had done their best for her, and Hallie could not find it in her heart to blame them for proving unable to change their own lifelong beliefs and behavior, and to move ahead with the times.

But, oh, how different things would have been if only her grandmother had never sent her away from Wolf Creek and Meadowsweet farm! A middle daughter, Gram had been the black sheep of the five Dewhurst sisters, estranged from her family because in her youth she had brazenly eloped with Jotham Taylor, Great-Aunt Agatha's fiancé.

The highly reserved, straitlaced Dewhursts had never forgiven Gram for that, her father remorselessly declaring her dead to them for her unspeakable sin, striking her name from the family Bible and cutting her off without a single penny.

Eventually Gram and her dashing, wayward husband had moved to faraway Wolf Creek and bought the small farm, Meadowsweet, where Hallie had been born and to which she was now returning.

She wondered how much both the town and the farm had changed in the intervening years since she had been gone. In her own mind, of course, both had stood still, frozen in time, just the same as when she had last seen them during her childhood. Still, she knew that in reality, that would not be the case, that both would no longer be as she remembered them.

Perhaps Wolf Creek had grown in size and population, become more than just a tiny dot on a road map, of little or no interest to passersby. Unlike some small towns, it had no claim to fame to attract tourists, to entice them off the beaten path to the single grassy square bounded on its four sides by the only main streets in Wolf Creek. In another time and place, the square would have been referred to as the village green. But Hallie recalled it only as the park where, on market days, she had romped with the other children, in the shadow of the town hall and the courthouse.

Not for the first time, it occurred to her how strange it was that her memories of Wolf Creek were so much clearer than those of Meadowsweet, her birthplace and the farm that had been her childhood home until her mother had died and Gram had sent her away.

Hallie remembered that the farmhouse itself dated from the 1800s and boasted Victorian architecture, and she had a vague impression of cupolas and towers rising from a large house whose lightning rods were silhouetted like needles against a boundless azure sky. But try as she might, she did not recall more than that, not even the color of the house's traditional wood scallops, siding and ornate trim, although she thought there had been at least three shades of paint.

More easily brought to mind was the sweet expanse of meadow whence the farm had taken its name. It had boasted a gay riot of grasses, toadstools and wildflowers, as well as butterflies, dragonflies and honeybees, the latter of which her grandmother had raised on the farm. All year long, when the weather had permitted, Hallie had played in the meadow, creating a vivid, imaginary world there, in which the insects were faeries and the toadstools and blossoms, their homes.

Even now, if she closed her eyes and tried very hard, she could still smell the sweet scent of the meadow and feel the warmth of the bright sunshine that had streamed to the earth there.

Reminiscing about that meadow had been her one salvation in those early days back East. It had been the place to which she had escaped in her mind when the unexpected loss of her mother, the sudden uprooting from her home and Gram, and the darkness and dreariness of the town house belonging to Great-Aunts Agatha and Edith had proved far too depressing and overwhelming for her, a lonely, baffled child.

But now, as all these memories of the meadow besieged her, Hallie could not suppress a wry smile. She did not think her great-aunts had ever believed in faeries. But Gram and Hallie's mother had believed, and they had passed that belief on to her.

They had talked to the honeybees, too. She wondered if those precious insects were still raised at Meadowsweet, their white wooden hives lined up neatly in a row behind the farmhouse. She hoped so.

Despite all the years that had passed since she had left Wolf Creek, there was still so much Hallie did not know, did not understand. Why, for instance, had Gram ever sent her away to begin with? Other children lost their parents, grieved and tried to go on with their lives afterward. They were not packed off to long-estranged relatives and never permitted to come back home. Still, that was exactly what Gram had done to her.

Had Hallie not been so certain of her grandmother's deep and abiding love for her, she would have thought that after her mother's death, Gram had not wanted to be bothered with her, a seven-year-old child. But, no, that was not the reason. Hallie felt sure of that. There was something else, something her grandmother had never told her, always keeping her at arm's length ever after, when the two of them had previously been so close.

Even now, when so much else was misty in her mind, Hallie could remember trotting in Gram's wake, helping to feed the chickens and to care for the honeybees, to harvest fruit from the orchard and vegetables from the garden and to hang the clean wash out on the clothesline to dry. Yes, there had been a time when she could have been described as her grandmother's little shadow.

But then her mother had died, and everything had changed.

Maybe because she resembled her dead mother so much, she had been a painful reminder to her grandmother of their mutual loss. Perhaps that was why it had appeared Gram could no longer bear the sight of her and so had packed her off to the care of Great-Aunts Agatha and Edith. If that were indeed the case, Gram's action would at least be understandable, if not particularly kind. Still, however plausible, this rationale did not seem at all in keeping with what Hallie recalled of her grandmother's joyous, generous nature. Nor did it explain why, in the end, Gram had willed her the farm.

But what other reason could there have been?

Hallie did not know, but one of the main reasons she was now returning to Wolf Creek and Meadowsweet was to try to find out. Her grandmother was dead and buried now, so could no longer keep her away, and surely, by leaving her the farm, Gram had intended that she come home at long last, anyway.

Because she was so lost in her thoughts, it was only at the last moment that from the corner of her eye, Hallie glimpsed the streak of dark fur that suddenly shot across the highway unwinding endlessly before her. Abruptly jolted from her reverie, she instinctively slammed on the brakes to avoid hitting the animal. In response, her small red vehicle screeched along the road, tires burning rubber and laying skid marks, before coming to such a bone-jarring stop that she felt certain she would have a bruise later from the seat belt she wore.

Ahead of her, in the middle of the highway, stood the largest wolf Hallie had ever seen.

As a child, she had often spied the animals, which had given Wolf Creek its name. But this one was unquestionably uncommon—and not only in size. For it was almost wholly black in color, with only a little silver-gray around its face, and as it stared hard at her, she saw that in a rare but recognized twist of genetics, it had retained the gleaming blue eyes with which all wolf cubs were born, but that normally turned golden in adulthood. A thin but visible jagged scar ran downward across its left cheek, as though the animal had survived some long-ago, hand-to-paw battle with a hunter and, for its defiance, been knifed during the desperate struggle.

Hallie felt strangely mesmerized by the beast's gaze, unable to tear her eyes away. Oddly, despite its obvious size and strength, the wolf did not initially appear menacing to her. But that was before, without warning, gathering its powerful muscles, it lunged toward her, abruptly leaping onto the hood of the car and pressing its muzzle against the windshield to peer in at her.

The unexpected weight and action of the animal jolted the vehicle violently, causing it to rock briefly and Hallie first to scream and then to catch her breath in her throat as she wondered if the beast were capable of somehow shattering the safety glass in order to attack her. Ludicrously, in some dim corner of her mind, she also hoped the wolf's hard, sharp toenails had not scratched the car.

The disjointed, upsetting thoughts that raced through her brain were joined by others equally unnerving. At this moment, the only weapon of any kind she possessed was the sturdy LifeHammer she carried in the glove compartment, in order to break the vehicle's windows in the event that she should ever have an accident that caused the car to become submerged in water. Still, she doubted the emergency tool would prove much use in defending her against the animal that loomed over her, panting against the windshield, its pink tongue lolling and its fierce canine teeth showing almost unnaturally white in the pallid, glimmering light that waned toward dusk.

Inside the car, Hallie could hear the sound of her own breath, now coming harsh and fast, and feel her heart hammering in her breast as she pondered her predicament. She had heard of bears climbing on vehicles and threatening their occupants, but she could not remember any news reports of wolves resorting to such behavior, and so she was at a loss as to how to proceed.

On sudden impulse, she blasted the horn, hoping to startle the animal and send it on its way. But much to her dismay, her thoughtless action did not seem to have any effect, and belatedly, it occurred to her that the sound might only enrage the beast, inciting it into attempting to destroy the thin glass barrier that was all that separated the two of them.

As her wide, apprehensive green eyes continued to be riveted on the wolf, Hallie could see that behind it in the distance, the thunderstorm that had earlier massed on the horizon was now beginning to roll inexorably eastward, its ponderous dark gray clouds billowing and spreading like giant, smothering cotton boles across the land. In between the titanic, madding clouds, the last vestiges of the pale, sickly sunlight shimmered, thin bony fingers stretching toward her portentously before mutely evanescing, swallowed by the descending twilight and advancing storm.

At the sight, Hallie felt her heart sink. She had hoped to be safely ensconced at Meadowsweet before the storm broke. Now perhaps she would not reach the farm at all.

Still watching the predatory animal hulking on the hood of the car, she covertly unlatched the glove compartment and groped inside for the LifeHammer. She knew that because the windshield was laminated glass, the emergency tool would not smash it. Rather, it was designed to break the tempered glass of the side windows to effect escape.

Nevertheless, she had some vague notion that if she beat authoritatively on the windshield, the beast might mistakenly believe she was not only armed, but also quite capable of defending herself, and would move on.

That, instead, it might perceive her gesture as a threat and try to attack her through the glass, Hallie did not even want to consider.

Nor did she even think about stamping on the accelerator and speeding away. Whether such a result would actually occur, she worried that the impetus of that act might fling the massive wolf savagely against the windshield, shattering it, thus giving the animal access to the inside of the vehicle and causing her to run off the road, at the very least.

She did have her cell phone with her and knew she could call the highway patrol for help. But what if dispatch did not believe her? Even as she tried to envision how to explain her situation, Hallie recognized how wild and improbable it would sound to someone not actually present to witness it.

She might be dismissed as some teenager pulling a silly prank.

Further, even if her story were given any credence, the animal would surely be gone by the time the highway patrol managed to arrive.

No, she was literally on her own. This particular stretch of road was desolate in more ways than one, without even another car in sight.

After rummaging blindly through the glove compartment for what seemed like minutes but, in reality, could only have been seconds, Hallie found the LifeHammer at last. As her fingers closed around it, they trembled with the fear that coursed through her wildly, and a lump rose in her throat, choking her. With determination, she swallowed this last.

Then, grasping the emergency tool tightly, she raised her fist, poised to strike the windshield, in an attempt to scare off the predatory beast.

At that, much to her utter surprise and confusion, its carnivorous visage pressing so close to her own vulnerable one through the glass split into what, in a human being, Hallie could only have described as a wide grin.

Then, just as suddenly as it had sprung onto the hood of the Mini, the great black wolf leaped down, swiftly and silently disappearing into the oncoming darkness and storm.

Chapter 2

Memories

Meadowsweet Farm, Wolf Creek, The Present

For what seemed like an eternity after the wolf had vanished into the twilight, Hallie just sat there in the car, her fear only gradually ebbing to be replaced by overwhelming relief and astonishment at what had happened.

What had prompted the animal's bizarre behavior? she wondered, still shaking. Perhaps the beast was deranged—or even rabid! At this last thought she shuddered visibly, knowing there was no cure for rabies and her imagination conjuring horrible, vivid visions of what a mad, sick wolf might have done to her, had it managed somehow to break the windshield and attack her.

And the way it had grinned at her! In that instant the animal had appeared almost human, amused by her plight and her desperate determination to fend it off however she could.

Now, for the first time, Hallie vaguely recalled snatches of conversation she had overheard in her childhood, something about the beasts that prowled the copses and meadows surrounding Wolf Creek, that they were not merely wolves, but something more....

No, that was simply impossible, nothing but local superstition and old-wives' tales to scare naughty children, surely—although at this particular minute, Hallie could almost believe the stories were true.

Shivering, she finally realized she still clutched the LifeHammer in her hand, and that the first drops of rain that presaged the impending storm had started to fall, splattering like the saliva from the wolf's panting tongue against the windshield. She could not continue to remain here on the highway, like a startled deer frozen in the oncoming glare of a pair of deadly headlights in the darkness.

Opening the glove compartment, she replaced the LifeHammer. Then, slowly, she stepped on the accelerator, only to discover that, sometime earlier, she had mechanically and habitually slid the gearshift into Park, so she had not had to keep her foot on the brake to prevent the vehicle from accidentally lurching forward with the animal atop its hood.

After slipping the gearshift back into Drive, Hallie started onward. But she had hardly picked up any speed at all when she suddenly observed a large, deep, dangerous pothole on her side of the road and drew once more to a halt.

Originally, the crater had been visibly marked with an orange-and-white-striped wooden barricade topped with flashing amber lights. But at some point, someone had obviously struck the sawhorse-shaped hazard warning, knocking it flat into the ditch alongside the highway.

Had Hallie come barreling down the road at her previous rate of speed, it was quite possible she would never even have noticed the blinking lights half concealed by the tall grass of the verge. She would have hit the pothole hard and dead-on, doubtless suffering a blowout or other serious accident.

If not for the wolf's unexpected and still-inexplicable intervention, she might even have been killed!

At the dreadful realization, Hallie felt an icy tingle run down her spine.

Gram had always taught her that the earth's creatures were a good deal more sentient than most people ever gave them credit for being. Had the animal somehow known what lay ahead of her in the road? Could it possibly have been attempting to save her?

No, surely, that was a farfetched idea!

Still, now that she thought about it, Hallie recognized that the beast had not actually done anything to threaten her. It had only stopped her dead in her tracks, forcing her to proceed a great deal more slowly when she resumed her course.

Oh, it had been a long day's worth of driving, and she was hungry, tired and letting her wild imagination run away with her, Great-Aunts Agatha and Edith would most certainly stoutly insist. Hallie had little difficulty at all in envisioning their severe expressions of disapproval and dismay, respectively—Agatha stern and unrelenting, Edith flustered and upset that there should be any discord in the town house.

So, for a very long time now, Hallie had kept

such fanciful notions as these to herself. But it seemed that the closer she got to the farm, the more her childhood self was struggling to emerge from the strict, sheltered cocoon in which the great-aunts had enshrouded it. For a moment, Hallie wondered if when she finally arrived at Meadowsweet, she would metamorphose into one of the bright butterflies that inhabited it. Then she shook her head, smiling ruefully at herself.

Great-Aunts Agatha and Edith would certainly not have approved of that idea!

But Gram would have. She would have flung her head back in that wholly unselfconscious and uninhibited way she had about her and laughed— a deep, rich laugh filled with the earthiness of the land she had loved so well and to which she had been so close.

At the memory, Hallie felt her eyes suddenly flood with tears, and for the second time in less than an hour, a lump rose in her throat, choking her. Abruptly, she laid her head on the steering wheel and cried her heart out.

But after a short while, she recognized that she must somehow pull herself together and get moving again, that at best, another vehicle might come along at any time and, not realizing she was stopped on the highway, crash into her.

Besides, there were the imminent storm and darkness to consider.

Determinedly stifling her sobs, Hallie carefully maneuvered around the treacherous pothole and at last drove on, eyeing the shadowy sky anxiously through the windshield. She loathed being caught in a storm while on the highway, and she suffered from night blindness, as well.

What if she missed the lonely and poorly marked dirt road that was the narrow turnoff to the farm? She certainly did not want to get lost out here in the middle of nowhere—especially with that huge wolf on the prowl!

Perhaps next time, it might not have such honorable intentions as she had so whimsically sought to bestow upon it.

Once or twice, from the corners of her eyes, Hallie uneasily thought she spied it following her, its silky black fur flashing amid the seemingly ceaseless rows of the tall cornfield that ran along one side of the highway. But as the dusk and the rain partially obscured her vision, she could not be sure, and resolutely, she told herself she was only imagining it, that for one thing, there was no way the animal could keep pace with her traveling car, and that for another, even if the beast were crazy and diseased, rather than sane and protective, it would scarcely be stalking her, but, rather, some other prey.

Still, briefly, she did wonder if there might be something about the color of her vehicle that had initially attracted the wolf and perhaps, more down to earth than her earlier flighty musings, even accounted for its odd behavior. The car was painted a vibrant crimson shade dubbed "Nightfire Red" by the manufacturer, and Hallie knew the color red was supposed to enrage bulls—at least, that was why matadors employed crimson capes in the bullring, although some said the hue was to disguise the bloodstains engendered by the brutal sport.

But because she had never heard anything mentioned about the color red inciting wolves, she was finally forced to discard the idle theory, eventually putting the entire episode down as a life mystery she would probably never solve.

Sighing deeply at the thought of other life mysteries that decision brought to mind, Hallie pressed on, wondering again why Gram had ever sent her away from Meadowsweet.

The rain was falling harder now, making it difficult for her see. So she switched on her windshield wipers and headlamps, once more hoping she did not miss the lane that led from the highway to the farm.

Keeping one hand on the steering wheel, she reached for the map she had printed out for herself a couple of weeks ago, her route carefully marked so she would know the way. Hallie had thought that once she neared the farm, her memories would kick into gear and serve to guide her home.

But she was also realistic enough to realize that it had been many years since she had seen Meadowsweet, and that memories sometimes played tricks on one, too. So, with the practicality instilled in her by Great-Aunts Agatha and Edith, she had taken the precaution of arming herself with the map.

She ought to be getting very close now, she thought. But in the end, despite everything, she still almost missed the turnoff. It was now so overgrown that she did not recognize it, and in fact, it was only the glare of her headlights shining on the badly askew signpost at the junction that caught her attention as she flew past.

"Dammit!" Hallie swore heatedly under her breath to herself.

Hitting the brake pedal, she screeched to a halt, glancing over her shoulder to be certain no one was coming. Then she backed up and turned onto the narrow, sandy lane, cursing some more as the Mini bounced along the bumps and ruts that riddled the ill-kept rural route.

Beneath the trees lining the road and forming a half canopy above, it was much darker than it had been on the highway, and in response, she turned on her high beams, totally grateful that the farm could not be much farther now.

Looking at the gnarled old branches of the thorny hedge-apple trees that rustled and whipped in the rising wind, Hallie knew she needed to reach Meadowsweet and batten down the hatches before the full fury of the storm was unleashed upon her.

A tornado might even be brewing, and she would have no way of knowing. Frowning at her own stupidity, she flicked on the radio, trying to tune it to one of the local channels. Instead, static and then rock music blasted into the Mini, and after a moment she gave up, switching the radio off, knowing she needed both hands on the steering wheel.

The rain pelted in splotches against the windshield, and once, a hedge apple was ruthlessly torn from one of the trees and hurled down to skitter like a poorly thrown bowling ball across the lane. Hallie could only feel relieved that the fruit had not struck her car.

As she watched the hedge apple roll off the road into the ditch alongside, her headlamps lit up a weatherbeaten sign hanging by one rusty chain from the barbed-wire fence to which it was attached. It read "Meadowsweet Farm."

Spinning the steering wheel quickly, Hallie turned onto the narrow, serpentine drive that led up a small hill to the old farmhouse beyond. Her heart pounded with anticipation, and her nerves went taut as she quivered with a strange mixture of trepidation and excitement.

Leaning forward, she strained for a glimpse of her childhood home, wishing she had arrived much earlier, when she could have seen it much more clearly.

Still, abruptly emerging from the windblown trees onto the hillcrest, she spied the house at long last, looming ahead in the darkness, illuminated by a sudden, jagged flash of scintillating lightning that forked across the churning sky.

Much to her dismay, the first unbidden thought that came into her mind as she instinctively paused the car on the knoll was that the Victorian farmhouse looked like something straight out of a horror movie. She suspected it would have been right at home next door to Norman Bates's creepy old house on the hill.

Silhouetted against the night sky, it was all dark, towering cupolas and pointed turrets capped with lightning rods that seemed to pierce the very firmament. As she caught sight of these last, Hallie felt some long-forgotten memory unexpectedly stir in her brain, and she heard herself as a child speaking to her grandmother in the expansive front yard.

"I don't like the lightning rods, Gram. They look like needles stabbing into God's eye."

And in her mind, as had happened in her childhood, she saw Gram throw back her head and laugh, and heard her declare, "Shout at the Devil, and spit in God's eye! That's just the way I've lived my whole life, Hallie—standing on my own two good feet, working with my own two strong hands, and never asking either man or beast for anything. And I don't mind telling you, it's been a long, hard path to follow, child. But in the end, I reckon it's a journey that's been the making of me, and I'm too old to change now, besides."

"Don't you believe in God and the Devil then, Gram?"

"Of course, I do, Hallie. It's merely that I've never noticed that either one has ever been of much use to humankind. Why, most of the wars in this old world have been fought in God's name, and if the Devil hadn't got into people, making them do evil to one another, I don't know what has.

"Sometimes, it seems like there's not a lick of

common sense or kindness or caring left on this entire earth! We were put here to take care of this planet and the creatures on it, you know, and it seems to me that between God and the Devil, we've done a mighty damned poor job of it all.

"No, child—" Gram had shaken her head firmly to emphasize her point "—I rely on myself, and what I know to be right and wrong according to the dictates of my own conscience, to lead my life, and I leave God and the Devil to those who need them. I hope that one day, you'll understand that and do the same."

Standing there with Gram in the yard that summer's day, Hallie had not truly comprehended a single word of their conversation. But now, the full meaning of their dialogue dawned on her, and in that moment she grasped her grandmother's character with far more clarity than she could ever have done in her childhood.

"Gram—" Hallie spoke now, her words breaking the stillness inside the car "—I don't know why you ever sent me away after Mom died. But I know you must have had a good reason, one you thought was right, just as you must have had one equally as good for bringing me home again. And while I'm not sure I've made up my mind yet about God and the Devil, I do have faith and trust in you.

"So…here I am, Gram, home at last after all these long years. I wish…I really wish you were here, too, standing on the front porch to greet me, the way you used to when you heard the school bus drop me off at the bottom of the hill. Instead, you're dead and buried in your grave, and I've got to rely on myself, just as you did.

"Oh, I guess I'll manage somehow. You see, I know how to stand on my own two good feet, too, Gram. Still, I've got to tell you that sometimes, like this evening, that's pretty damned cold comfort. What I wouldn't give for a cup of your hot Earl Grey tea, served with your smile and words of wisdom, right about now. Maybe if I'm lucky, there'll still be a tin, at least, somewhere on one of your kitchen shelves. I can only hope."

With that last thought to sustain her, Hallie put the gearshift back into Drive and guided the vehicle on toward the old farmhouse that stood waiting silently for her, a momentous sentinel in the rainy darkness, relentlessly defiant against the blustering wind—and armed with needles that still dared to jab the thunderous sky.

Chapter 3

Home Is Where the Heart Is

By the time Hallie pulled the car to a stop beneath the intricate wooden carport on one side of the house, the wind was lashing the trees unmercifully, the rain was pouring down and the fleeting dusk had well and truly died.

She was inordinately grateful for what protection, however small, the carport provided as, with difficulty born of the storm, she lifted the vehicle's rear hatch and unloaded the two bags she had packed to bring with her. Then she fumbled in her purse for the house keys Gram's attorney, Simon Winthorpe, had mailed to her some days ago.

Once she had finally got the side door open and stepped into the small vestibule beyond, she felt for the light switch on the wall. But much to Hallie's consternation, when she flicked it, nothing happened. Either the electric company had not received her instructions to restore the power, or else the storm had knocked the power out. Either way, she was obviously not going to be able to get the lights to come on.

Wondering what else might go wrong this seemingly ill-omened night, she set her luggage inside, then returned to the car to fetch the flashlight from the emergency roadside kit she always carried in the cargo space. Punching one of the buttons on the key remote, she locked the car, then ran back into the house, closing the door behind her, shutting out the inhospitable elements.

For a moment, Hallie just stood there in the darkness, dripping with rain and shivering with cold. She correctly suspected that the outside temperature had dropped twenty degrees or more in the last few hours, and she was dressed for summer, not for the onslaught of a storm and its attendant chilliness.

But finally, collecting herself, she switched on the flashlight and began to explore the house. Once or twice, she tested other light switches, only to receive the same disappointing result as before. She had hoped the lightbulb in the vestibule was simply burned out, but now, it was clear to her the power itself was indeed off.

As she proceeded down the hall beyond the vestibule and then through several of the rooms on the ground floor of the house, shining the flashlight this way and that, Hallie was swept with myriad emotions.

Much to her vast relief, in so many ways that she now realized had subconsciously been of prime importance to her, the old farmhouse had not changed. In rooms that had clearly been redone over the years, Gram had chosen the very same patterns that had always papered the walls, and she had reupholstered the furniture with fabric identical to the worn material it had replaced. She had moved little or nothing in the intervening years. Sofas, chairs, curio cabinets, and tables still stood where they always had, and paintings still hung in their accustomed places.

The large portrait of Hallie's mother, Rowan—forever young and beautiful—still looked down at her from its place of honor above the intricately carved fireplace mantel in the front parlor.

On the much simpler fireplace mantel in the back parlor, Gram's treasured collection of antique Victorian oil lamps were still clustered, along with the sharp, ornate brass scissors she had used to trim the flat wicks, and the beautiful, matching brass box that housed the stick matches she had employed to light them.

Now, as in her childhood she had watched her grandmother do so many times before, Hallie crossed the room to remove the oil lamps' glass chimneys, carefully trim the wicks and set them ablaze. Soon the back parlor was awash with the warm glow of their flames and with the fragrant scents of the oils that filled the glass fonts. Sweet lavender and vanilla mingled with the pungent smell of the beeswax with which her grandmother had always polished the furniture.

Standing there in the room, closing her eyes and inhaling the old, familiar aromas, Hallie could almost imagine she was a child again, that any minute now Gram herself would come into the back parlor, wiping her hardworking hands on the apron she had always tied on over her simple workaday garments.

But, no, Hallie would never see her grandmother again in this life.

At the thought, hot tears stung her eyes, and almost, she wondered if she had made a terrible mistake in coming back here to Meadowsweet.

It was said that one could never go home again.

Sighing heavily, fighting back the flood of tears that threatened once more to fall, Hallie abruptly switched off her flashlight. Then, picking up one of the oil lamps, she made her way to the kitchen.

There, she drew up short, stunned and incredulous.

For here, at last, everything was changed.

Once, solid-oak cupboards, turned dark with smoke and age, had lined the walls, one of which cabinets had sported an ancient copper sink, and open shelves cluttered with crockery had hung above. There had been a large, worn butcher block in the middle of the room, and a badly scarred yellow pine floor. The open hearth to one side had been composed of reddish brown bricks blackened with soot from winter fires.

The kitchen was the one part of the house Hallie remembered much more vividly than all the rest. It had always reminded her of the old cozy but mysterious kitchen in some fairy-tale cottage, and sometimes, she had half suspected Gram herself was really some enchanting witch.

But now all that was gone, as surely as her grandmother was. In its place were clean white beadboard cupboards topped with black granite counters, above which gleamed glass-fronted upper cabinets. A white porcelain Belfast sink had replaced the copper one, and a long wooden farmhouse table occupied the center of the room. The floor was now a checkerboard of black and white tiles, and the old brick fireplace had been painted white to match. Against one wall stood a massive Welsh dresser Hallie had never before seen. Only Gram's crockery on its shelves was the same. Even her old stove and refrigerator Hallie thought must surely have dated from the fifties had given way to modern reproductions that looked like Victorian antiques.

What on earth had ever caused her grandmother to make such drastic alterations to the kitchen, Hallie wondered, deeply puzzled, when she had plainly left the remainder of the house so largely untouched?

As she continued to stare at the many changes that had been made, Hallie was suddenly beset with the oddest sensation that there was something missing, something she ought to have been seeing, but that was no longer there in the kitchen. But try as she might, she could not think what it was, and at last, she gave up the attempt, realizing it was getting late and that she was truly hungry and exhausted.

There would be plenty of time in the weeks to come to explore the old farmhouse properly during the daylight hours—and when she had got the power to the lights restored.

Fortunately, Gram's sweeping redecoration of the kitchen had not included switching from a gas stove to an electric one, so Hallie would be able to cook, at least. Now, if she could only find a tin of tea and something to eat.

She had planned to run up to the corner market upon her arrival and buy some groceries. She had not counted on oversleeping earlier at the motel where she had spent last night and, as a result, getting such a late start today. Nor had she accurately calculated how long the drive this afternoon would take or on being delayed by the storm and the wolf.

So much for the best-laid plans of mice and men, she thought, frowning.

Opening the icebox, Hallie was once more besieged with amazement and disbelief. For, instead of finding it completely empty, as she had expected, she discovered it was filled with food: a huge glass platter of cold fried chicken and large ceramic bowls of homemade baked beans, cole slaw and potato salad—precisely what Gram herself would have prepared for her homecoming.

At first, in her weariness, Hallie thought dimly that it must be victuals hospitable neighbors had made and carried over when her grandmother had died. Then she recognized how stupid that notion was, that there would have been no one here to provide meals for and that Gram had passed away last month, besides. All the food would have spoiled by now.

Adding to her confusion were the plates of biscuits and brownies she finally noticed sitting on the counter next to the fridge. Slowly unfolding the plastic wrap and examining them, she found they were fresh, probably baked that very afternoon, in fact.

At the realization, Hallie felt a sudden cold chill creep down her spine.

Someone had been in this house earlier—perhaps was even still here....

From the knife block perched on the farmhouse table, she carefully withdrew a sharp butcher knife for protection. Then, picking up the oil lamp, she embarked upon a thorough inspection of the house, determinedly pushing aside her nostalgia and grief at familiar sights that kindled long-buried memories to concentrate instead on some sign of an intruder.

Back through the ground floor, she progressed, her mouth dry and her heart pounding as she searched behind sofas and yanked open closet doors to peer inside, only to find nothing save emptiness. Then, stealthily, Hallie ascended the beautifully carved staircase in the main hall to the upper story.

Here, the tale was exactly the same as it mostly was below. Nothing had changed, except that just like downstairs, all the closets were bare. Much to her astonishment and heartache, even her old bedroom looked just as she had left it so many years ago, all her childhood books, dolls and stuffed animals perched neatly on their shelves, her robe still lying across the foot of the bed.

At the sight, Hallie felt more certain than ever Gram must have had a very good reason for sending her away. Her grandmother would never have left this room untouched like this if it had been nothing more than an annoying reminder of a bothersome child, or if Hallie's resemblance to her dead mother had been more painful than Gram could bear.

Now there remained only the attic. But when she reached the bottom of the narrow staircase that rose to that dark space above, Hallie hesitated, all the strictly forbidden Gothic stories she had ever sneaked into her great-aunts' town house and read as a teenager returning to haunt her. She had always thought those poking-and-prying heroines who had invariably crept up steep narrow attic stairs to investigate matters that really had not concerned them in the first place were exceedingly dumb. A deranged killer had always been hiding up there, lurking in the shadows, lying in wait to conk the heroine on the head as a dire warning for her snooping.

Most assuredly, Hallie did not want to suffer a like fate. She had already had more than enough for one day, and now, it belatedly occurred to her that Mr. Winthorpe's wife, Blanche, had probably brought the food over and left it for her. It was just the sort of neighborly gesture Mrs. Winthorpe would have believed proper. Hallie did not know why she had not thought of it earlier, instead of leaping to the crazy conclusion that an intruder was in the house.

For pity's sake! she chided herself sternly. An interloper wouldn't have stocked the fridge and baked biscuits and brownies! She must be even more tired than she had realized.

Sighing with relief, truly glad she was not to be compelled up into the attic, Hallie returned downstairs to the kitchen, inordinately grateful she was not going to be forced to cook for herself, either. She even discovered a tin of Earl Grey loose tea in one of the cupboards and so was able to make a cup of hot tea.

Perhaps her luck was changing, after all.

Filling a plate, she ate mechanically, now so weary that she could actually scarcely eat at all. Still, she knew she needed something in her stomach if she did not want to awaken with a sick, hunger headache in the morning. So she cleaned her plate and drank her tea.

When she had finally finished, Hallie unconsciously did something she had not done since her childhood in this very kitchen: she swirled the remnants of her tea around clockwise three times, then turned her white ceramic mug upside down on its matching saucer to drain off the remaining liquid.

For an instant she waited expectantly for Gram to take the cup and turn it right side up again, peering into it to see what symbols the tea leaves left inside it had formed. But of course, her grandmother was not there, and so Hallie could not imagine why she had ever done such a thing, indulging in a long-forgotten gesture Great-Aunts

Agatha and Edith had labeled "superstitious pagan nonsense" and a habit they had labored diligently to break her of.

"Aunts Agatha and Edith would surely not be very happy with me right now, Gram." Hallie spoke in the empty room. "They said it was a good thing you sent me to them, that otherwise I might have lost my way and become a heathen and a sinner, just as you did. I know they meant well and loved me. Still, it was a long, hard path you set my feet on, Gram, when you sent me away to them. Did you know it would be? Is that why you did it? You always believed that kind of journey was the making of a person."

There was no response save for the plaintive keening of the wind outside and the steady thrumming of the rain against the kitchen windows. But Hallie had not really expected one. In some dark corner of her mind she knew she was talking only to herself, that her grandmother had passed beyond the pale into another state of being.

Still, for old times' sake, and for everything from her childhood in this farmhouse that she held dear, she closed her eyes, made a wish then upended her teacup to look inside.

She supposed there were symbols someone like Gram, knowledgeable about the art of reading tea leaves, would have recognized. But to Hallie, the dregs seemed like nothing more than a complete mishmash at the bottom of her cup.

Inexplicably, she felt a strange, bewildering sense of disappointment, as though she had believed her grandmother would somehow speak to her through the teacup—and had not.

Shaking her head at her own foolishness, she smiled wryly.

"What a silly notion, child!" she could hear Great-Aunt Agatha announce firmly. "If they are good, the dead go to Heaven. If they are evil, they go to Hell. What they do not do, missy, is hang around the world from which they have departed, carrying on in death just as they did in life! It was undoubtedly Henrietta who put such a heathenish idea into your head. She ought to be ashamed of herself! But, then, I'm certain she is not, no— for she has never suffered any shame at all at her wild behavior, no matter how grievous it has proved to her poor family!"

"Henrietta" had been Gram's given name. Hallie was named after her.

Covering her mouth, Hallie yawned widely, dully realizing she was so thoroughly exhausted that she was about to fall sound asleep sitting straight up in her chair.

"Well, Gram, as much as I'd like to continue this somewhat lopsided conversation, I'm afraid I really do need to get to bed. I can hardly keep my eyes open."

In fact, Hallie was so tired that instead of washing the dishes, as she normally would have done, she set her cup and plate to one side of the sink. Then, after extinguishing all the oil lamps in the back parlor, she turned on her flashlight to guide her in the darkness and trudged back upstairs, not even bothering with her luggage.

She would unpack tomorrow, when she was rested and feeling more herself. Right now, she had the most peculiar sensation that by coming back here to Meadowsweet, she had somehow been mysteriously transported back in time to her childhood. She was thinking, saying and doing things she had not thought of in years—and talking to herself, besides.

What she needed was a long hot bath, followed by a nice soft bed.

But in the end, Hallie skipped the former and, stripping off her clothes, headed straight for the latter in her childhood bedroom.

Her last thought as she drifted into slumber was that somewhere outside in the night, a lone wolf was howling in the storm.

Chapter 4

Reading the Tea Leaves

When Hallie awoke the following morning, it was to the raucous noise of a rooster crowing and a bell chiming.

For a moment, still half asleep and disoriented by the sight of the room that met her drowsy gaze, she mistakenly believed she was a child again, and she waited expectantly to hear Gram's footsteps in the main hall below and the muffled sound of voices as the door was answered.

Then, abruptly coming to her senses, Hallie remembered she was a woman fully grown and that her grandmother was dead. Jolted into action, she reached for the alarm clock on the night table, only to realize she had never set it the night before, so that was not what was ringing. It must be her cell phone. But, no, she had left that in her purse downstairs last evening.

It really was the front doorbell chiming, then, just as she had initially surmised.

Leaping from her childhood bed, Hallie hastily dragged on the same crumpled clothes she had so tiredly discarded the night before, then combed her fingers roughly through her long blond hair. She supposed that even so, she looked a fright, and she wondered who could possibly be here at this early hour.

Then, glancing at the alarm clock, she realized it was half past ten, that the morning was well advanced, that it was she who was late, rather than the hour that was early.

Not bothering with her shoes, Hallie scrambled down the stairs in the main hall, reaching the front door just as the bell rang again.

"Gram!" she cried, stunned, as she opened the door and spied the elderly lady standing on the wide wooden verandah.

"Oh, dear, I fear it never even occurred to me

that you would mistake me for Henrietta, child," the older woman announced, obviously flustered by the error, shaking her hatted head and clucking with disapproval at herself. "How very stupid and thoughtless of me! What a shock it must have been to you to see me, then. No wonder your poor, lovely face has gone so very white. I'm so sorry. You'll have to forgive me for being such a foolish old woman!

"I'm Gwendolyn Lassiter, Henrietta's younger sister—and I do apologize if it seems presumptuous of me, child, but after all these years, well, I'm old and so I probably don't have much time left, and I thought it was high time we finally met!"

"Aunt…Aunt Gwen…yes…yes, I can see, now, that you're not Gram—although you do look a lot like her! I should have realized, but I—I just awoke, you see," Hallie confessed. "So I'm afraid I'm not at my best."

"Oh, dear," Aunt Gwen reiterated ruefully. "I didn't think about the fact that you might still be in bed, either. But I expect you were worn out from your long journey. I can't believe you drove all the way here from back East—and all by yourself, too! You must be a very brave and resourceful young woman. Is that your little car I saw under the carport? But it must be, of course.

It's darling. Well, aren't you going to invite me in, dear? Or did Aggie and Edie succeed in convincing you I am as dreadful a black sheep as they always thought Hennie was?"

As she spoke, the elderly lady's faded blue eyes twinkled with delight, and a mischievous dimple appeared in one cheek, so Hallie got a glimpse of what she must have been like as a child and could not repress an answering grin.

"I think maybe you were only a gray sheep, Aunt Gwen!"

At that, the older woman's laughter tinkled brightly.

"Well, I can't say I find that very gratifying," she declared stoutly. "For I think I would quite like to have been painted just as black a sheep as poor Hennie was. So scandalous and exciting, you know—although I daresay that in this day and age, one's elopement with the fiancé of one's sister would scarcely raise even an eyebrow, much less start a decades-long family feud!"

"No, I don't suppose it would," Hallie agreed, holding open the screen door. "Please forgive my momentary lapse in good manners, and do come inside, and tell me how you came to be here."

"As to that, Hallie, for the past several years, since my husband passed away, I lived here with

Hennie—right up until the day she died, of course. But at her death, Meadowsweet became yours, so I didn't feel it would be right of me to go on staying here at the farmhouse—especially when you might not even know I still existed. So I moved into Wolf Creek's one and only bed-and-breakfast."

"Oh, Aunt Gwen, you needn't have done that," Hallie insisted as she led her great-aunt into the kitchen. "I wish I'd known you were here, but Gram never said a word about it to me. I wonder why."

"That was my fault. I fear I'm a bit of a coward, child, and I simply didn't want Aggie and Edie to learn I was here. They would have believed I had sided with Hennie against them, and they would have written me off, just as they did her.

"Such a real pity, it was, that they decided to go on holding their grudge against her for the rest of their lives, when we all might have been friends. But there it is. I suppose that in the end, they had simply held on to their bitterness for so long that they just couldn't let it go—not that there was ever any true justification for it, of course.

"It was always Hennie, not Aggie, poor young Jotham Taylor had come to the town house to court, and it was only Father's wholly archaic notions about the eldest daughters being married before the younger ones that caused him to try to foist Aggie off onto Jotham. But, then, Father had been born during an earlier century and era, so he was very straitlaced and highly principled, and he refused to waver. Eventually, he succeeded in maneuvering poor Jotham into offering for Aggie instead, but naturally, once that deed was actually done, both Jotham and Hennie were miserable. So, finally, they decided to cut their losses and elope."

"I never knew that—the whole story, I mean...only bits and pieces," Hallie said, fascinated by this peek into her family's past. "It really *was* too bad of Aunts Agatha and Edith to hold such a terrible grudge, then. But, from the things she did impart, I feel quite certain Aunt Agatha, at least, was firmly convinced in her own mind that Gram stole Jotham away from her."

"No, doubt." Aunt Gwen's voice was wry. "It's just like Aggie to have deluded herself in such a fashion."

"Have you eaten yet, Aunt Gwen?" Hallie asked, abruptly recalling her manners. "Would you like some breakfast? Oh!" She drew up short. "I've just now realized it must have been you who left supper for me last evening."

"Good heavens! Don't tell me I forgot to give

you my letter, too!" The elderly lady fumbled in her purse, eventually withdrawing a crumpled envelope marked "Hallie." "I did. Oh, dear, I'm so terribly forgetful these days. That's what comes of growing old. Yes, it was I who brought the food, and I intended to leave you this note, explaining everything. You poor thing! No wonder you were so confused this morning and mistook me for Hennie!

"I'll tell you what, Hallie—" Aunt Gwen removed her wide-brimmed straw sun hat, laying it on the old farmhouse table "—I ate at the bed-and-breakfast. So why don't I make you breakfast instead, while you go upstairs and get cleaned up? If you don't mind me saying so, child, it looks as though you slept in those clothes, and I noticed you hadn't unpacked your baggage, either.

"There are a few other things that need to be taken care of here this morning, besides, which is one of the other reasons why I came. There are still some chickens here at Meadowsweet, which need feeding. I didn't know, of course, what you would want done with them, whether you intended to stay here permanently, making the farm your home, or whether you meant to put it on the market. So I was reluctant to sell the chickens or even to give them away. But that's why Old

Bernard is still screeching his darned fool head off outside. He's hungry."

"Old Bernard?" Hallie raised one eyebrow inquisitively.

"The rooster," the older woman explained. "I know it's awful, but Hennie said he was so mean that she was going to name him after Father—and I'm afraid that's just what she did!"

"Good grief," Hallie rejoined lamely.

Still, she was unable to repress the laugher that bubbled from her throat, and soon Aunt Gwen was giggling as hard as she.

"I'm sure...poor Father...must have turned over in his very grave...when Hennie christened that old rooster," the elderly lady said, in between bursts of merriment.

"Well, I don't believe Gram was ever a highly reverent sort of person," Hallie mused aloud, remembering. "I guess perhaps she had got her fill of that growing up. Are there still bees here at Meadowsweet, as well, Aunt Gwen?"

"Oh, yes, dear. Hennie would never have parted with her bees. In fact, right before she died, she said it was more important than ever to keep them going here at the farm, that for some unknown reason, billions of honeybees are dying all over North America. 'Colony Collapse Disorder,' it's called, she told me. Without bees to pollinate our crops, many will be lost. I don't know all the particulars myself, but I suppose it could lead to all kinds of food shortages and maybe even a worldwide famine. I don't think anyone really knows for sure."

"Well, we'll continue to take care of the bees here at Meadowsweet, then," Hallie stated firmly, "and see that they don't die."

"Are you going to remain here, then, for good, Hallie?" the older woman inquired.

"I'm…I'm not certain yet."

"Is there some reason why you can't? I mean, I know from what Hennie told me that you have both a job and a husband somewhere back East—"

"No." Hallie shook her head. "Well, at least, not a husband…not anymore, anyway. In the end it…it just didn't work out. Before she died, Aunt Agatha tried to tell me it wouldn't. But I just thought she was so bitter about not ever having got married herself that she wanted to ruin my own happiness, too. So I didn't listen to her. But I should have, because everything she ever said about Richard— that's my ex-husband—eventually turned out to be true. He wasn't the right man for me and was never going to be."

"You're divorced now, then, I take it?" Aunt Gwen's tone was sympathetic.

"Yes...yes, we're divorced now. In point of fact, I signed the papers just before I left to come here. But that didn't matter. Our marriage had been over for quite a while. I guess I just hadn't wanted to face it. But now, I think perhaps that's one of the main reasons I decided to come back here to Meadowsweet. I needed some time to myself, a quiet place to lick my wounds. So I took a sabbatical from my job—I'm a graphic designer—and I packed my bags, and well, here I am."

"And now I've thoughtlessly intruded on your solitude." The older woman sighed deeply. "I'm so sorry, Hallie."

"No...no, you needn't be," Hallie said adamantly. "In fact, I'm glad you're here, Aunt Gwen. Naturally, I've heard about you now and then over the years, but with the family being what it was, most of them on such ill terms with one another, you and I just never seemed to have a chance to meet, to get to know each other."

"Yes, I know, and of course, it didn't help that until these past years, I was never around much, but usually traveling out of the country somewhere," the elderly lady noted. "That's why I always missed holidays, birthdays, weddings and funerals, and the like. My late husband, Professor Victor Lassiter, was an archaeologist, you see. So we were invariably off in some far corner of the world, digging up old ruins and artefacts—besides which, as you said, our family was never particularly close."

"Still, what an exciting life you must have led, Aunt Gwen."

"Yes...yes, I have. Still, I don't mind telling you there's a lot to be said for putting down roots and making a real home someplace permanent, instead of always living in a tent and out of a suitcase."

"It must have been upsetting for you, then, to move from Meadowsweet, when you had doubtless finally made a home here," Hallie observed. "Please come back, Aunt Gwen. Had I known you were here, I would never dreamed of letting you move out. Besides, I could really use your help with the farm, I know. There's so much I'll need to relearn. Why, if you hadn't shown up, Old Bernard might have starved to death this morning. And I would very much enjoy your company and getting to know you. Really, you're all the family I have left now, and I expect...I expect it will seem very lonely here at Meadowsweet without Gram, besides."

Much to her dismay, Hallie felt the sudden tears that seemed to come so easily of late sting her eyes.

"I miss Hennie, too, child," Aunt Gwen averred softly, patting Hallie's hand comfortingly. "There isn't a day that goes by that I don't think about her. I'm so glad she and I were able to become such good, dear friends before her passing, the way sisters ought to be. I very much regret, now, that I didn't have the same chance to accomplish that with Aggie and Edie before they were dead and buried, too, and of course, our youngest sister, Isabelle—Belle, we always called her—contracted tuberculosis and died before she was yet twenty. Doctors didn't know as much about treating it in those days as they do now.

"But...enough about the past for now. We'll have plenty of time for all the old stories in the weeks to come. Oh, I'm so happy to have met you at long last, Hallie!" Aunt Gwen hugged her great-niece quickly but lovingly. Then she went on.

"With your permission, I'll move back today—to tell you the truth, I was so hoping you'd ask me to do just that. I do miss this old farm—more than I had ever thought possible—not to mention how Lucy Bodine, who owns the bed-and-breakfast, is about to drive me clean around the bend. I don't know whatever made that poor woman believe she could operate a business. She's got about as much common sense as one of Meadowsweet's chickens."

Moving to the kitchen sink, Aunt Gwen began to run the water, clearly intending to wash the dishes Hallie had neglected last evening.

"Oh, Aunt Gwen, you don't have to do that," Hallie objected. "I was so exhausted last night that I left that mess, and I meant to clean it up this morning. And in all the excitement of meeting you, I don't think I ever thanked you properly for the supper, either. It was delicious, and you can't imagine how grateful I was for the tin of tea, either."

"Don't think another thing about it, dear. I was glad to do it—and I'm delighted you're not actually bent on becoming a hermit, besides, because I can see from your teacup that you're soon going to have another visitor!"

"You...you can read my tea leaves?"

"Why, yes." The older woman nodded. "Hennie taught me. You see this stem here? That's a man, a stranger, who's going to come calling in the near future. And that heart there...that represents love and romance, just exactly as you might imagine. Did you wish on the cup last evening, after you'd drunk your tea?"

"Yes," Hallie admitted.

"Good—because that star on the rim means

that whatever you wished for is going to come true. So I hope it was a good wish, and not something wholly frivolous." Aunt Gwen smiled, her pale blue eyes sparkling once more and her dimple peeping. "I know how you young people are nowadays, wishing you had a better car or more cell-phone minutes or other such things. Do you play video games, as well?"

"Sometimes," Hallie responded, grinning sheepishly.

"Well, good!" Aunt Gwen avowed, much to her niece's surprise. "Maybe you can teach me how to play—or, at the very least, how to manage the accounting software Hennie and I bought for the computer. She and I couldn't make heads or tails of it. But, oh, we did have such fun trying.

"Now, for heaven's sake, Hallie, go and get cleaned up, while I cook your breakfast, so we can get those chickens fed before I'm thoroughly tempted to go outside and strangle Old Bernard for making such a dreadful racket!"

Chapter 5

Talking to the Bees

Grabbing her luggage from the small vestibule beyond the kitchen, Hallie headed upstairs to her childhood bedroom. She yearned desperately for a long hot bath, but settled instead for a short steaming shower in the main bathroom. Then she brushed her teeth and hair, plaiting this latter into a French braid, thinking that would prove more practical for farm chores than leaving it loose. She dressed in clean clothes—a T-shirt, jeans and a pair of sturdy old shoes she would not mind getting muddy, then rejoined her great-aunt in the kitchen.

By that time, breakfast was ready, consisting of fresh eggs from the chicken coop, along with bacon and Texas toast from the sack of groceries Aunt Gwen had thoughtfully brought with her this morning and had fetched from her car.

Although both women would have loved to linger over tea, there were the chickens to be fed and other chores to attend to, and soon the two of them were tramping around the farm, with Aunt Gwen pointing out a number of different things she and Gram had intended to do before the latter had so suddenly and unexpectedly passed away.

"This is where Hennie died," the elderly lady explained as they finally reached the white wooden beehives that lay just beyond the backyard. "One minute, she was talking to me and the bees, and the next minute, she was suffering a sudden, massive stroke.

"I knew what it was, of course, the moment I saw it happen. My late husband died in much the same way, except from a heart attack, rather than a stroke.

"I reached her side just in time to hear her whisper Jotham's name, and then she stretched out one hand—toward nothing, it seemed, when I looked in that direction. But I knew he was there, that he had come for her at long last, and when I glanced back down at her, she was gone.

"I suppose most people would think it a curious thing, Hallie, but she was smiling. So I knew she was happy and at peace when she finally left this world, and that she'd gone just as she'd always intended—suddenly and out here among the beehives. Hennie was always so proud about standing on her own two good feet, and she never wanted to become a burden to anybody. That would have been soul destroying for her, I think."

"Yes, I think so, too." Hallie nodded in agreement. "I just wish...I just wish I'd been able to see her again before she died. After Gram sent me away back East, she never let me return here. She invariably claimed it would only anger Great-Aunts Agatha and Edith, but somehow, I always had the oddest notion that that wasn't the real reason. Still, why Gram would lie to me, I simply can't imagine."

"No, neither can I," Aunt Gwen said firmly. "So I'm sure it was just as Hennie told you, dear. Having taken you in, Aggie and Edie truly would not have been happy about you shuffling back and forth between their house and Hennie's farm—for the simple reason that they would never have been quite sure just whose side you were really on, as awful as that may sound."

"Yes…yes, I can understand that. Still, Gram was my grandmother, and I loved her, and after that day she drove me all the way into the city and put me on that plane, I never saw her again. Oh, every year she always claimed she would come visit me, but she never did. I knew she wouldn't, of course, that she'd never leave this farm. But in later years, after I was grown, I would have been more than glad to make the trip to Meadowsweet, if she hadn't always had some excuse for putting me off.

"Growing up, I used to think maybe Gram just hadn't wanted to be bothered with me, because I was a child when Mom died. Then, once I became an adult and realized exactly how much I resemble my mother, I thought maybe Gram simply couldn't bear to look at me anymore, because I was such a painful reminder to her of her dead daughter.

"But after seeing my childhood bedroom last evening, that it was untouched and looked just the way it did when I left it, I don't believe either of those things is true. Nor do I understand why, after keeping me away from Meadowsweet for so many years, Gram would will me the farm. Did she mean for me merely to sell it, then, Aunt Gwen, without ever setting foot on the place again?"

"Oh, no, child. I don't think that was her intention. From all she used to say in that regard, I know Hennie always felt land was the only thing that truly endured and so it should always be passed down to the next generation, come hell or high water, no matter what. So I'm sure that's why she wanted you to have it, that deep down inside, she hoped you would settle down here and raise a family, just the way she did."

"But, then, why did she ever send me away in the first place?" Hallie queried, perplexed. "And why keep me away, even after I was grown?"

"I don't know, Hallie. You're asking me questions I can't answer. But whatever Hennie's reasons may have been, I'm certain they were good ones—and that she loved you dearly, besides. She read your letters time and again, and she had dozens of treasured scrapbooks she'd made over the years, filled with all the pictures you sent her. I'll show them to you later, if you like. She was so proud of you!"

As she observed the younger woman's obvious pain and confusion, Aunt Gwen's wrinkled, weatherbeaten face softened with sympathy and comprehension.

"There is one other thing Hennie did say once, which may be significant, child, and bring you some kind of peace of mind. She said…she said she had failed Rowan…failed to keep her safe, but that at least she hadn't made that same mistake with you. She said life with Aggie and Edie had made you strong and practical, a survivor, and that in the end, that was just as important as dancing with moonbeams, that she hadn't ever fully comprehended that before Rowan died."

Rowan was Hallie's mother.

"Mom had an accident. She tripped and fell down the stairs in the farmhouse, and broke her neck," Hallie stated slowly. "Poor, poor Gram. I never knew she felt that way—and it's not even true, besides! She didn't fail to keep Mom safe. Mom was a woman grown, with a seven-year-old child of her own, and her death wasn't Gram's fault at all. She wasn't responsible. Why, she wasn't even home when it happened!

"I was here that day, but Gram wasn't. She'd gone to the corner market that afternoon. So why she should blame herself for it, I can't imagine. Maybe Gram thought that if she had been here, she could somehow have prevented Mom's death. Still, I don't see how. It was just an accident…a terrible accident, that's all.

"I can't even recall much of anything about that day, you know. I've tried and tried to remember exactly what occurred, but it's all still just a blur. I was alone in the house with Mom's body for quite a while before Gram returned home, and because I was only seven at the time, I guess that must have been a truly traumatic event for me, so I've just blocked it all out."

"Oh, Hallie, it would have been for anybody, dear, but, yes, most especially for a child. Poor Hennie. She must have felt horribly guilty that she wasn't here when Rowan died—oh, not because she might have been able somehow to save her, because, as you said, what happened to your mother was simply a tragic accident, but because Hennie might have spared you from being alone for so long with your mother's body.

"Nowadays, in emergencies, young people just pick up their cell phones and dial nine-one-one. But we didn't used to teach children things like that, and of course, there weren't any cell phones back then, either—or, at least they weren't glued to people's ears, the way they are now." Aunt Gwen shook her head, frowning a little.

"Anyway, we're not going to learn the answers to all your questions this morning, child," she continued. "So let me show you a bit about the bees and how to care for them. Among other things, you must always remember to talk to them and tell them everything, of course! Then we'll run into Wolf Creek and pick up my belongings from the bed-and-breakfast—at least, I'm hoping you'll accompany me there. I confess I've had just about all I can take on my own of Mrs. Bodine's lunatic behavior."

"Of course I'll go with you, Aunt Gwen. We ought to get some more groceries, and I've got to find out what's happened to the power at the farmhouse, besides. I e-mailed Mr. Winthorpe that it should be turned back on prior to my arrival, but I think he must have forgotten about it, because there wasn't any last night. If the main bathroom didn't have those bright sunny windows, I'd have had to take my morning shower in the dark!"

"I wondered why the icebox didn't seem nearly as cool as it ought to be," the older woman said. "I turned the temperature inside it down, so it would get colder. I didn't realize the power was out, and I know it was on yesterday, that it was never actually shut off after Hennie passed away. So there was no need for Mr. Winthorpe to get in touch with the power company.

"The power must have been knocked out by the storm. That sometimes occurs, you know. A fuse winds up being blown in the breaker box—from the lightning, I suppose. I could be wrong, but I don't think the lightning rods guard against that. I think they're mainly to prevent the house from being set on fire by a lightning strike. Because the house is so isolated, sits on a hill and has all those soaring cupolas and towers, if it didn't have the rods, it would be a prime target for lightning.

"As you undoubtedly already know, Hallie, ours are made of good, old-fashioned copper, rather than the aluminum that's often used nowadays."

"Yes, I always thought they looked like giant needles, and I never liked them. But now that I'm no longer a child, I realize how necessary they are for protection from the kind of thunderstorm we had last night. Everything's so bright and peaceful this morning that it's hard to believe there was such a savage storm last evening. But there's not a single gray cloud in the sky today."

"No, it's a beautiful day," Aunt Gwen agreed. "Well, I think I've shown you just about everything that needs doing for the moment, dear—although I've undoubtedly forgotten something and will remember it just as soon as we get into town. But, then, if I can't recall it now, it surely won't be anything of much importance.

"Will you do the honors and drive us into Wolf Creek, Hallie? I'm dying to see the inside of your little car. It's just so cute! It's one of those new Minis, isn't it? I remember how popular they were years ago. I guess they've made a comeback now, haven't they?"

"Indeed they have, Aunt Gwen, and I just adore mine, so I'll be glad to drive us."

Companionably, the two women strolled back to the farmhouse to scrape the mud from their shoes and to fetch their purses.

As they had earlier observed, it was a gorgeous day. The sun shone brightly in the clear blue sky, its countless rays streaming to the earth already filled with heat, promising a steaming afternoon. The land all around the farmhouse was lush and green from its thorough soaking last evening, and it still smelled of rain, clean and fresh.

The house itself, seen in broad daylight, no longer resembled something from a horror movie, but, rather, was a highly impressive example of Victorian architecture, painted in deep shades of blue, green and plum to highlight its many outstanding features. The multitude of flowerbeds clustered around its brick foundation and beyond, in the yard, bloomed in a brilliant riot of color, and butterflies, dragonflies and bees flitted gaily from blossom to blossom.

"You never see anything like this in a city,"

Hallie remarked, as, plopping down on the wide wooden verandah, she took off her shoes and began to clean them. "I didn't realize how much I really missed it all until now."

"Yes, it's truly lovely and peaceful here, isn't it?" Aunt Gwen said. "Still, the sun can grow quite hot and fierce during the summer, so you really ought to have a sun hat, Hallie. Remind me about that when we're in town, and we'll stop at the discount store and buy you one. You've got such a beautiful complexion that it would be a shame if it wound up all tanned and wrinkled like mine."

"I don't believe I'd mind that too much, Aunt Gwen. I've never been particularly vain about my looks. As you can no doubt imagine, vanity was one of the many deadly sins Aunt Agatha railed constantly against. I'd originally believed there were only seven, but she had a list quite a bit longer than that."

"Poor Aggie." The elderly lady sighed. "I'm sure she wound up as austere as Father because she was the firstborn and so bore the brunt of everything in our household when we were growing up. Edie was the next oldest of us, and I'm certain she would have turned out quite differently if she hadn't always been under Aggie's thumb, because there was always a gentle sweetness in her that Aggie never had. Well, I hope they're both at peace now—and that, wherever they may be, they've both made their peace with Hennie, as well."

On that note, the two women went inside the house, Hallie running barefooted up the stairs to her childhood bedroom to exchange her sturdy shoes for a pair of attractive sandals.

Strangely, when she reached the landing, she felt a sudden, inexplicable chill, as though a goose had just walked over her grave. Then, as light as feather, something brushed against her cheek, sending an icy tingle down her spine.

At first, Hallie thought she had walked into a cobweb, and she raised one hand to dash it away. That was when she spied the pale gray mist drifting across the landing. For a long moment it seemed to her that it bore the shape of the great black wolf and then that of a man. Then, in the next instant, the mist crept stealthily down the stairs to disappear without warning beneath the threshold of the front door, and Hallie couldn't be certain she had actually seen anything at all beyond a trick of the sunlight streaming in through the upstairs window on the landing.

Still, puzzled and perturbed, she shivered a little as she made her way to her bedroom to grab her sandals. If she didn't know better, she would think she had just seen some kind of a ghost or something.

She had just gone back downstairs to join Aunt Gwen in the kitchen, for a tall cool glass of lemonade the latter had made, when the front doorbell rang.

"That's probably Blanche Winthorpe," the older woman announced. "She told me she was going to drop by sometime today, to be sure you'd got here safely and to see if there was anything you needed."

"Or, maybe," Hallie teased, grinning, "it's that tall, dark, handsome stranger you warned me about when you read my tea leaves."

"Now, now, I don't remember issuing a warning—or saying anything about him being tall, dark *or* handsome, either!" Aunt Gwen insisted, her faded blue eyes filled with merriment and her dimple showing. "So that's nothing more than wishful thinking on your own part, child!"

"No." Hallie shook her head, still smiling. "I'm done with men—at least for a while. Besides, if it really *is* the visitor you promised, he's probably fat, bald and ugly! That's just the kind of luck I seem to have these days, you know," she called back over her shoulder, as she headed toward the main hall.

Still chuckling to herself, she opened the front

door wide—only to draw up short, her breath catching in her throat, at the sight that met her suddenly wide green eyes.

Chapter 6

The Arrival of the Stranger

The man standing on the farmhouse's verandah was indeed tall and dark—and quite possibly the handsomest man Hallie had ever seen.

He had shaggy, silky black hair, touched lightly at the sides with silver-gray, and within his tanned visage, a pair of startlingly blue eyes gleamed beneath swooping black eyebrows. An aquiline nose was set above full, carnal lips and a strong, determined jaw, and a thin, jagged scar marred his left cheek, as though sometime in the past, he had become embroiled in a barroom brawl and fallen prey to the blade of his opponent's knife. His deeply tanned skin had a slight coppery cast to it, as though there were American-Indian blood in him somewhere.

Obviously a man in the prime of his life, he wore a plain black T-shirt from which the short sleeves had been ripped to leave his powerful, muscular arms wholly bare, and the cotton fabric of which stretched tightly across his broad chest and lean waist, revealing not even a single ounce of fat. A pair of snug, button-fly black jeans encased his long, corded legs, and black boots were upon his feet. In one hand, he held a black Stetson hat that had clearly seen better days.

"Ms. Muldoon? Ms. Hallie Muldoon?" the stranger drawled, his voice low and throaty, almost like a growl, as, spying her, he raised one eyebrow inquisitively and somehow provocatively. "My name's Trace Coltrane. I've been doing a lot of work over at Farmer Frank Kincaid's place, Applewood—" he mentioned the name of a neighboring farm "—but that's all finished now, and he said as how you had just come back to Wolf Creek and so might be needing some help here at Meadowsweet.

"I don't charge much…just room and board

and a hundred dollars a week, and I'm a hard worker—not one of these soft slack kids you mostly see around nowadays. I can turn my hand to just about anything, from mending fences to breaking horses, and I'm neither a drunk nor a gambler, so you won't need to worry about me not showing up on time or not at all.

"Ma'am, is something wrong? You've not spoken a single word, and the way you're staring at me, I'm beginning to think I've suddenly grown two heads or something!"

"No...no, it's not that." Hallie swallowed hard, attempting to collect her wits. "It's just that I'm experiencing the strangest sensation that I've...that I've seen you somewhere before. Have we ever met, Mr....ah...Coltrane? No, forget I even asked that question—because if we had, I'm sure I'd remember. Still, you seem familiar to me somehow."

"I certainly can't imagine why, Ms. Muldoon."

The stranger's face was politely impassive, but for some unknown reason, Hallie abruptly had the oddest feeling that he was inwardly laughing, and that, somehow, she had missed a joke she should have got.

"Are you a longtime resident of Wolf Creek, Mr. Coltrane? Perhaps you're someone I recall from my childhood. I was born here, you see, even though I've not lived here for many long years now."

"No, ma'am. I'm just drifting through, trying to earn a little money as I go along. Even if he's rootless, a man's still got to eat—and keep a roof over his head. I noticed your barn's in sad shape, so could use some work. Still, it's got an old tack room that would suit me just fine as a place to bunk if you agree to hire me.

"So, what do you say, Ms. Muldoon? Will you give me that job or not?"

The wheels in Hallie's brain churned furiously. From her tour of the farm this morning, she already knew there was far too much heavy labor that needed doing for her and Aunt Gwen to accomplish it on their own, and she also knew she was unlikely to find anyone else who would do the work for room, board and a hundred dollars a week.

Still, she hesitated. Despite the bizarre sense of familiarity she continued to experience as she gazed at him, Trace Coltrane was, in reality, a stranger to her, and by his own admission, he was nothing more than a drifter, besides, just passing through town. What if he actually possessed wicked designs upon Meadowsweet and her and Aunt Gwen, meant to rob them or worse?

"I'd need references, Mr. Coltrane—one from Mr. Kincaid, at the very least," Hallie stated firmly.

"Of course, ma'am." Trace nodded. "I expected no less."

"We can phone Frank Kincaid, Hallie, if you like." Aunt Gwen spoke behind her in the main hall. "Hello, Mr. Coltrane. I'm Gwendolyn Lassiter, Hallie's great-aunt. I apologize if I seem to have been eavesdropping. But when it didn't appear to be Blanche at the front door, after all, Hallie, I grew curious and a trifle concerned.

"At any rate, I'm sure Mr. Coltrane's all right. It was I who mentioned your homecoming to Frank in town the other day and that if you intended on staying at Meadowsweet, you'd undoubtedly need some help. So I know Mr. Coltrane's been laboring at Applewood for quite some time now, and believe you me, Frank's not the easiest person in this world to please. In truth, he's rather an old curmudgeon.

"So I feel certain he could find little fault with Mr. Coltrane or his work—and as you are now well aware, we really could use some assistance here at Meadowsweet, dear. I'm afraid the place has gone rather downhill these past years, becoming way too much for Hennie and me to manage on our own. We fully intended to hire some outside help this summer. But of course, after Hennie passed away, I was reluctant to do anything without your permission and until I knew what you meant to do with the farm."

"Yes, very well, then, Mr. Coltrane. Because my great-aunt has vouched for you, the job's yours if you want it—but naturally, I will place that call to Mr. Kincaid, simply as a matter of course."

"That's fine with me, Ms. Muldoon," Trace replied laconically, as though he could not have cared less.

But once more, Hallie suffered the strange sensation that he was laughing inside, and really, it was most unnerving to her. Despite her great-aunt's endorsement—and the evidently notoriously irascible Mr. Kincaid apparently approving of the stranger, also—she felt Trace Coltrane might well prove insufferably arrogant, and she suspected he would be a dangerous man to cross, too.

For all his outward affability, she sensed an alertness and tension about him, as though he were habitually on his guard, poised to spring like some predator upon its prey.

At that thought, Hallie abruptly realized whom—or, rather, *what*—the stranger reminded her of, why he seemed so familiar to her. He bore an uncanny resemblance to the huge black wolf that had leaped upon the hood of her car last night—right down to the silky silver-tipped black hair, the striking blue eyes and the facial scar.

What were the odds, she wondered, that an animal of that unique description should have run out in front of her car the previous evening and that a man bearing those very same characteristics should show up on her verandah this morning—especially right after that strange mist she had seen on the landing?

Unbidden, the frightening tales she had heard in her childhood about the beasts that populated Wolf Creek being something more than just mere wolves again returned to haunt her.

Was it possible Trace Coltrane was a werewolf?

No, even the very idea was ridiculous! Hallie remonstrated herself sternly. There were no such thing as werewolves. They were nothing more than mythical creatures, made to appear actually to exist by tales told about them by ignorant peasants of bygone centuries, who had not understood congenital generalized hypertrichosis, a rare disease in which the patient suffered an abnormal, excessive growth of hair, thus resembling, some claimed, a wolf.

Or perhaps the stories stemmed from the practices of ancient cultures who had donned animal skins during celebratory pagan rituals, pretending to become the beasts they portrayed.

Really! Ever since she had returned to Meadowsweet, Hallie's wild imagination had run away with her in ways it had not done since childhood. Truly, she must get hold of herself and stop all these fanciful indulgences.

"Aunt Gwen and I were just on our way into town, Mr. Coltrane," she explained. "So perhaps you could start work first thing tomorrow morning."

"There's no time like the present, I've always thought, Ms. Muldoon. So I'd be more than happy to begin right now. If you'd like, I can start by driving you and your aunt into Wolf Creek. I assume that because you've only just arrived at Meadowsweet, you will, among other things, be picking up groceries, so there might be some heavy stuff I can help with.

"I'm afraid my pickup truck's seen better days—" with one hand, he indicated the battered old vehicle parked on the circular gravel drive "—and wouldn't prove very comfortable for either one of you ladies. But I notice you've both got cars—and to be honest, I wouldn't mind taking a spin in that Mini."

For the first time, Trace grinned—a wide, devastating smile that crinkled the corners of his deep-set blue eyes and showed even, white teeth.

It was a pleasant, friendly and yes, very sexy grin, Hallie mused—honest enough with herself to admit she found Trace Coltrane a highly attractive man. Still, his smile reminded her vividly of the way she had thought the wolf had grinned at her, and so she was also assailed with another wave of uneasiness.

Had she made an awful mistake by hiring the stranger?

He might not be a werewolf, as she had so ludicrously imagined just moments past. Still, there were other kinds of wolves....

"Why, how very kind of you to offer," Aunt Gwen said. "Hallie and I would be more than pleased to have you drive us, wouldn't we, child? I'm sure Hallie has driven so much these last few days that she would be grateful just to be a passenger, and to tell you the truth, I'm much more comfortable nowadays if I don't have to drive myself, either. When one gets old, no matter how hard one tries, one's wits and reflexes just still aren't ever as fast and sharp as they are in one's youth, are they?

"Come along, then, Hallie. You don't mind if Mr. Coltrane drives your car, do you? I'm sure your insurance policy covers anyone whom you give permission to drive your vehicle. Most of them do these days, if that's what's worrying you."

"No, I'm not bothered, Aunt Gwen. I'm just…still a little tired from my long trip, that's all. I'm quite happy to have Mr. Coltrane drive us." Hallie handed him her keys.

"Please. Call me Trace. I'm not in the habit of standing on formality," he declared. "Why don't you ladies wait here, while I fetch the car."

As he loped off toward the carport on the side of the house, Hallie turned anxiously to her great-aunt.

"I sure hope you're right about that man, Aunt Gwen," she said. "Because I really would hate to see my car suddenly speeding clean away from here without us!"

"Oh, good heavens, dear! I sincerely doubt Mr. Coltrane is a car thief! Trust me. There is simply no way Frank would have employed anybody like that. No, I'm certain everything will be fine. Indeed, Mr. Coltrane seems like a very nice young man…most handsome and personable, in fact— although I do so like to see a man dressed up, rather than down. But of course, it wouldn't be at all practical to wear a suit for farming chores.

"So, while I surely wouldn't want to be placed on a par with Aggie and Edie, child, I can tell you haven't lost the vivid imagination Hennie used to say you'd been blessed with, and I think perhaps it wouldn't hurt to err a bit more on the practical side. No offense intended, dear."

"None taken. Oh, Aunt Gwen, I've been telling myself pretty much the same thing for the past two days! I don't know what's the matter with me. Ever since I came here, I've felt somehow as though I were only seven years old again…imagining all sorts of highly improbable things…things I know full well are simply ridiculous. Why, if you heard some of what I've thought, you'd no doubt believe I'd taken leave of my senses. It all started with that damned wolf!"

"What wolf, dear?"

"I'll tell you all about it when we get home. I don't want Mr. Coltrane to think he's come to work for a real nutcase. If there's one thing at all I remember about Wolf Creek, it's that everyone in town knows everybody else's business, and I certainly don't want people believing I need to be locked up in a mental hospital someplace."

"Oh, I wouldn't worry about that, child. I'm sure that half the time they all thought that about Hennie. She just used to laugh and say she hoped she gave them something to talk about, that otherwise their lives would be pretty darned boring."

There was no time to speak further, as just then, much to Hallie's vast relief, Trace pulled up in her vehicle, clearly having had no intention of absconding with it.

Jumping out, he courteously opened the two passenger doors for the women, and somehow, despite all her protests that Aunt Gwen would surely be more comfortable in the front seat, Hallie wound up sitting there instead.

"I'm surprised you didn't get a manual six-speed transmission with this Mini," Trace remarked as he deftly maneuvered the vehicle around the circular drive and then down its winding length toward the narrow dirt lane that led to the highway into town.

"I thought the automatic would be more practical for me," Hallie explained. "It's a continuously variable transmission with Steptronic control, so I can choose between the usual automatic mode and a six-gear semiautomatic transmission. The former makes driving in city traffic a whole lot easier, and before I returned to Meadowsweet, I did a great deal of that. The latter is for sportier operation. To try it, just switch the gear from D to S. I confess I hardly ever do so myself, I'm just so accustomed to using the normal automatic."

"Well, I'm afraid it's all Greek to me!" Aunt Gwen declared, chuckling. "But it is certainly a very attractive little car. I can see why you fell in love with it, Hallie. If I were many years younger, I'd be tempted to buy one myself. You know, now that I think about it, I believe I saw one of these cars in a movie once. Actually, there were two or three of them, as I recall, and they were used to transport a large load of stolen gold bars. I always wondered how vehicles that small could carry all that weight."

"It was called *The Italian Job*—the movie, I mean, Mrs. Lassiter," Trace said, "and in it, the thieves had the three Minis professionally modified in order to handle the weight of the gold bars."

"I see. I must have missed that part somehow. When one gets to be my age, one usually can't hear as well as one used to, so I often miss much of what's going on in a movie. Because of that, I'm so glad I can watch the subtitles for the deaf on cable television."

"We have cable TV at Meadowsweet?" Hallie asked, somewhat bemused.

"Oh, yes, dear. Time has marched on here at Wolf Creek, just as it has everywhere else in the many years since you've been away. We have a laptop computer and a high-speed connection to the Internet, too, at the farm. Did you think we were still pumping water by hand and utilizing an outdoor toilet?"

"No, Aunt Gwen." Glancing over her shoulder to the backseat, Hallie grinned at the elderly lady. "We were never *that* backward, even when I was a child."

"But you did have some idea that we'd been somehow frozen in time, that the progress made by the rest of the world had somehow passed us by?"

"I suppose just a bit," Hallie admitted sheepishly.

"I've never known why people who live in big cities invariably seem to have the mistaken belief that everybody else is still living in mud huts." Trace spoke wryly. "Like, if something doesn't happen in a major metropolis, it's not of any consequence. To my mind, that's a thoroughly dumb and dangerous way of thinking."

"How so?" Hallie inquired, a trifle dryly, wondering if the man were actually insulting her or merely speaking in general terms.

"Well, let's just take a couple of diseases like AIDS and Ebola, for example," he went on. "They didn't initially break out in any large city, but, rather, in rural Africa. But it wasn't until they migrated out of those areas and into cosmopolitan ones that anybody outside of a handful of medical and scientific specialists sat up and took and any real notice. Yet the global repercussions of those diseases—particularly where AIDS is concerned—have been devastating."

"Yes, that's true," Aunt Gwen agreed. "My late husband, Professor Lassiter, used to say much the same thing. He'd point to disease and famine, earthquakes and tsunamis, customs and cultures, all kinds of things that originally appeared to affect only a small region, but that eventually wound up producing worldwide consequences. He was an archaeologist, and I assisted him with his work, so we both saw how easy it was for entire civilizations simply to disappear from the face of this planet."

Tiredly, Hallie closed her eyes, allowing the sound of their conversation to wash over her unimpeded. She was glad her great-aunt's own good etiquette dictated carrying on a polite dialogue with Trace Coltrane, because right now, Hallie wasn't sure she could have managed it.

She felt the man—whether consciously or not—had been ill-mannered, at best, with his observations about big cities, especially since he knew she had journeyed straight from one to Meadowsweet.

But at the moment she simply did not care, felt

far too weary to take up the gauntlet he had perhaps thrown down before her. In truth, she was grateful not to be the one driving them into town. The past few days of doing nothing but driving had taken their toll on her, and she had not been fully rested when Aunt Gwen had inadvertently wakened her this morning.

Surreptitiously, from beneath the thick fringe of her sooty lashes, she briefly watched Trace and knew she need have no fear he was not a capable and expert driver. Her car was in good hands, unlikely to be driven recklessly into a ditch or a head-on collision.

Thus satisfied, after a moment, with the bright yellow sun beating down on her warmly through the windshield, Hallie slipped drowsily and inexorably into slumber.

Chapter 7

Wolf Creek

"Ms. Muldoon. Ms. Muldoon—Hallie—wake up! As much as I'd like to permit you to continue sawing logs, Sleeping Beauty, I can't leave you out here, locked in the car in this heat, and I need to help Mrs. Lassiter with her luggage, as it appears Lucy Bodine's wayward grandson is nowhere to be found on the premises of her bed-and-breakfast."

Starting wide-awake, Hallie abruptly sat up straight in the passenger seat, glancing around wildly, momentarily completely disoriented by her totally unfamiliar surroundings.

She had been dreaming—about the massive black wolf that had leaped upon her car—and at this instant, all she knew was that it had somehow managed to shatter the Mini's windshield, to open the passenger door to loom over her, preparing to spring. Its dark, scarred visage was now pressed ominously near her own pale, tremulous one, its breath warm against her skin, one paw grasping her shoulder, shaking her in a way that was not particularly gentle.

Terrified, she screamed loudly.

"Oh, for Christ's sake!" Trace swore, baffled and dismayed.

Then, not knowing what else to do, he swiftly clamped one hand over Hallie's mouth, covertly looking around to be certain no one was paying attention.

"Please, Ms. Muldoon...Hallie...please, be quiet! I'd sure hate for everyone in town to get the wrong idea here, and I really don't want to wind up spending the night in jail for something I didn't do. I was only trying to waken you—not rape you or something, for crying out loud! Are you fully awake now? Do you comprehend what I'm saying to you?"

Mutely Hallie nodded, and slowly Trace removed his hand from her soft, generous lips.

"I'm...I'm so sorry," she whispered, her lovely countenance still ashen. "I didn't realize I'd fallen asleep. I—I was having a bad dream...a-a nightmare, and for a minute I didn't know where I was or who you were... I'm so sorry," she reiterated lamely.

"It's all right. I understand. I'm just glad you're all right, that you don't think I was trying to hurt you or anything." Trace paused. Then he continued. "I wouldn't have disturbed you, but as I said, I can't leave you locked inside the car. It's got so hot outside now, that I don't believe even cracking the windows would help. I still think you'd be dead in a matter of minutes.

"Further, although I know Wolf Creek's a small town and so has very little crime, I was also very much loath to leave you asleep with the car windows rolled down. Anyone might have snatched your purse, at the very least. I know some of the teenagers around here are from the wrong side of the tracks and so probably wouldn't hesitate to resort to that."

"Yes, you're no doubt right about that. Where's Aunt Gwen?"

"She's already gone inside the bed-and-breakfast to collect her belongings. I told her we'd be along in a minute, once I'd woken you. She'll need help with her baggage."

"Yes, I remember now. You said Lucy Bodine's grandson wasn't anywhere around. He's the de facto bellboy, I take it."

Finally pulling herself together, Hallie unfastened her seat belt and picked up her purse, hesitating only when Trace offered his hand to assist her from the vehicle. As though well aware of her brief discomfiture, he flashed a sudden, sardonic—and, to her, wolfish—grin.

"I assure you, Ms. Muldoon, I don't bite," he drawled.

"Mr. Coltrane, I think perhaps you do," she blurted thoughtlessly.

Hearing that, Trace threw back his head and laughed heartily, while Hallie blushed furiously, thoroughly mortified at having said such a thing.

"All right. I confess that under the right circumstances, I might be tempted to indulge in a nibble or two," he told her, still grinning impudently. "But, somehow, the parking lot of Ms. Bodine's bed-and-breakfast doesn't exactly conjure the proper mood—especially with her peering through the front window at us!"

"Good grief!" Hallie frowned, dismayed. "She

must be as nosy as she is featherbrained! *There's* one of the drawbacks to rural living, Mr. Coltrane. Everybody in town knows everyone's else's business. In big cities, nobody cares."

"That's right. They don't. You can be brutally murdered in broad daylight on a busy street, and people will simply step over your corpse to get wherever they're going."

"Well, I suppose there is a grain of truth in that," she conceded, giving him her hand at last, so he could her help from the car.

Trace's fingers, warm and strong, closed around her own, sending a sudden, unexpected wild tremor coursing through her as he pulled her from the vehicle to her feet. For a moment, she swayed against him giddily, inadvertently making contact with his broad, muscular chest. In that minute, it was as though lightning leaped between the two of them. His hand tightened on hers.

"Steady...steady there, Ms. Muldoon." He spoke, his voice low and husky. "I wouldn't want you to trip and fall. I don't think this gravel would be very good for those gorgeous long legs of yours."

"I wasn't—I wasn't aware you'd noticed my legs, Mr. Coltrane," Hallie said, swallowing hard.

"Believe me, Ms. Muldoon, I've noticed. I

generally don't miss much—particularly when there's a damsel in distress involved."

"I assure you, Mr. Coltrane, I'm neither a damsel nor in distress."

"Aren't you, Hallie? Well, we'll see. And it's Trace. As I told you before, I don't hold with standing on formality."

"All right, then…Trace. Why don't you go and help my great-aunt with her luggage? You see, I've always found it's best not to mix business with pleasure, that there's a definite line that ought to be firmly maintained between employer and employee."

At that, sighing ruefully, he reluctantly released her.

"Well, I reckon I've got sense enough to know when I've been put in my place," he observed, mockingly tipping his black Stetson hat to her. "Thank you so much, ma'am, for reminding me I'm only the hired help."

With that shot, he turned to swagger into the bed-and-breakfast, leaving Hallie to follow in his wake, her heart thumping far too fast in her breast.

Dammit! She did not want to be attracted to Trace Coltrane!

She had already made one dreadfully stupid mistake by marrying Richard Forsythe—who had ultimately proved to possess every single fault Great-Aunt Agatha had so direly predicted. Hallie certainly did not now wish to make another poor error in judgment, especially when she was just recovering from that initial heartbreak, bent on becoming her own woman again.

That was one of the reasons why, upon her divorce, she had resumed her maiden name, Muldoon. She wanted no painful reminders of the past.

Equally, she wanted no enticing promises of a future that might eventually prove just as disastrous.

She was much older and wiser now, she hoped, than when she had first met Richard. And so, no matter how physically attractive Trace Coltrane might be, Hallie had sense enough to realize that a man who, by his own admission, was nothing more than a drifter was not the sort of stuff that ought to be considered prime marriage material.

Had she wished to indulge in a summer fling, she had no doubt he would fit the bill just fine. But Hallie had never been one to engage in frivolous affairs for her own amusement. When she gave of herself to a man, it was honestly and wholeheartedly, and she was not willing to settle for anything less in return.

Something told her that for all his apparent easy-going outlook on life, Trace Coltrane had erected barriers a mile high around his heart, and that these would not be easily demolished. She did not want to be the one to engage in the futile attempt.

No, even though he had taken offense at her words, she was glad she had made the situation between them perfectly clear.

After they had got Aunt Gwen and her baggage loaded into the car, they headed for the discount store, where Hallie succumbed to the elderly lady's urging and purchased a sun hat. They did the bulk of their grocery shopping there, as well, then, on the way home, stopped in at the old corner market that had been a hallmark of Wolf Creek for as long as Hallie could remember.

Much to her surprise, as they made their rounds, she realized the small town had not changed nearly as much as she had surmised it might have. The large grassy square at the heart of Wolf Creek still looked the same, as did the town hall and courthouse that bounded the green on two sides. Several old businesses had disappeared, of course, but new ones, including a cyber café, had sprung up to take their place.

The entire while, Aunt Gwen chattered brightly, pointing out this and that as Trace drove through what eventually turned into rush-hour traffic—although, to Hallie, it seemed the streets were hardly crowded at all.

"Now, that's Kiley Ebersoll's hair salon, Prime Cut, Hallie," the older woman said. "She's a real sight! She's always got pink or blue or green hair, and she's got so many holes pierced in her ears, I don't know why she doesn't just put one big one in her head and be done with it. Still, that's where all the young women your age go to get their hair done—not that I hope you're going to color yours bright burgundy or purple or any of these other unnatural shades so many young people these days seem so fond of, of course."

"No, I'm happy with what God gave me. Still, I'll need to have my hair trimmed now and again. So it's nice to know there's somebody here in Wolf Creek who'll be able to give me a good cut. Thanks, Aunt Gwen, I'll remember that place."

The corner market was scarcely any different at all from how Hallie recalled it. It still boasted the same old gravel parking lot and faded gasoline pumps out front, a wide wooden porch punctuated with an assortment of battered chairs, rockers, a checkerboard and an ancient, bright red Coca-Cola machine, an ill-fitting screen door and, inside, a big, old-fashioned pickle barrel and rows of apothecary jars filled with hard candy.

Hallie had used to come here with Gram early in the mornings, to fetch rashers of bacon and plastic cartons of milk for breakfast. At the thought, memories of her grandmother beating batter for pancakes crept into her mind, and she felt her mouth water, suddenly wishing she had a stack a mile high, dripping with maple syrup and butter.

For all its modern conveniences, the discount store could never compete with this old corner market, Hallie mused, with its narrow, cramped aisles and hodgepodge of stock seemingly crammed at random on the shelves. The corner market had time and personality on its side.

"Hallie…oh, Hallie, dear, I want you to meet Jenna Overton." Aunt Gwen interrupted her reverie. "I don't know if you remember her from your childhood or not. She works for Judge Newcombe, over at the courthouse."

"No…no, I'm so sorry. I can't say as I do," Hallie replied as she turned to greet the woman politely. "I'm Hallie Muldoon. Were you a friend of my mother's?"

"Not a close friend, but we attended school to-gether, of course, so I'd known her for many years before she died," Jenna explained, gazing hard at Hallie in such a strange way that it began to make her feel uncomfortable. "Please forgive me for staring," the woman went on, as though she had sensed Hallie's sudden discomfiture. "You resemble her so very much that it's almost like seeing a ghost!"

"Oh, of course, I didn't realize... I suppose I must initially have the same effect on people who knew my mother that Aunt Gwen had on me when I first saw her. She looks so much like Gram that for a moment, I mistook her for my dead grandmother."

"Yes, it really *is* a bit unnerving, isn't it, to think you're seeing someone you had thought long dead and buried?" With one plump hand, Jenna idly pushed her rather greasy, shoulder-length black hair back from her round, pudgy face. "Well, I need to get going. It was very nice meeting you, Hallie. Thank you for introducing us, Mrs. Lassiter. You ladies both have a nice day."

Clutching the sacks full of candy she carried, Jenna trundled through the crowded aisle toward the cash register up front, paying for her purchases, then exiting the corner market.

"She's such a queer duck," Aunt Gwen remarked as they glanced after the departing woman. "Hennie used to say that's what came of Jenna, having worked in that musty old courthouse since she was a practically a teenager, buried in reams of files, constantly at the beck and call of that pompous old goat Judge Newcombe!

"And of course, because she's apparently been heavy ever since she was young, all the children used to make a great deal of fun of her and of her last name, I understand, calling her 'Over a ton' instead of Overton, and other such unpleasant monikers. Kids can be so very cruel, you know.

"As a result, I don't think she's really at all good with people to begin with, and I believe that seeing you really did give her quite a turn. As you know, I never met your mother. So I've only the pictures I've seen of her over the years to tell me how much you look like her, Hallie. I guess I should have realized it would be different for those persons who actually knew her."

"Yes, I'm certain it must be. Anyway, I didn't think Ms. Overton was nearly as odd as some of the other people in town whom I've met today."

The elderly lady laughed.

"That's true. I suppose every small town has its own fair share of real characters. I know there are those in Wolf Creek who thought Hennie belonged in that category!"

Hallie grinned.

"Gram really *was* a character, Aunt Gwen—as well you know. Still, I know she derived a great deal of amusement from her own eccentricities. Half the time, I think she did things just to see how people would react."

"I wouldn't be at all surprised."

"As much as I hate to break up this little tête-à-tête—" Trace joined the two women in the aisle "—I've finished gassing up the Mini now. So we're good to go whenever you're ready."

"I think we're just about ready now." Hallie indicated her shopping basket, practically filled to overflowing. "So we'll cash out and join you in the car."

"As you wish," Trace said.

"Don't tell me—*The Princess Bride?*" she suggested impudently, smiling. "I take it you've seen that, as well as *The Italian Job?* Funny. You just don't strike me as a moviegoing sort of man, Trace."

"Oh, I like a good film as well as the next person," he drawled, his blue eyes gleaming in a way that, had she known him better, would instantly have put Hallie on her guard. "Maybe one of these nights, if you and Mrs. Lassiter would be interested, we can all take in a movie at the local cinema—my treat."

"Why, how very kind of you to offer, Trace!" Aunt Gwen cried, obviously as delighted as a child by the idea. "We'd enjoy that very much, wouldn't we, Hallie?"

"Yes…yes, of course," Hallie had no choice but to reply, realizing then how deftly she had been maneuvered into an outing she would otherwise have refused on principle. "You ought to be ashamed of yourself!" she hissed to Trace once Aunt Gwen had walked on toward the cash register up front. "I thought I made myself perfectly clear earlier."

"Don't worry, Ms. Muldoon. You did." He grinned at her in that cynical fashion that somehow reminded her eerily of the huge black wolf. "However, I was not under the impression that didn't mean we couldn't even be friends. And if you ask me, Hallie, you could badly use a friend right now—perhaps even more than you realize."

"What's that supposed to mean?" she asked a trifle defensively.

"It means that as I told you earlier, I don't usually miss much, and that for all the brave face you've put on everything, I think that deep down inside, you're really rather a lost lamb at the moment…uprooted from some big city, transplanted to a small town you haven't seen—maybe haven't even thought of—in years, grieving for your dead grandmother, determined to tackle the farm that was her legacy to you and set it to rights. That's a great deal for anyone to have on her plate. Under the circumstances, it would be quite natural to feel just a bit overwhelmed."

"I guess that I do," Hallie reluctantly confessed. "And so I apologize if I've seemed, well…as—as prickly as a porcupine."

"There's no one besides your great-aunt to whom you could turn for help? No Mr. Muldoon, for example?"

"Muldoon's my maiden name. And no, I'm not married—at least, not anymore—if that's what you're asking. How about you, Trace? Have you got a wife and kids someplace? Did they get to be too much for you, so you just upped and left, drifting on down the road?

"That's what my own father did, you know," she continued, a faintly bitter note in her voice. "He simply packed his bags one day and disappeared, leaving behind a couple of scrawled lines to Mom that having a wife and baby wasn't his cup of tea, after all. So I never even knew him, have no memories of him at all, merely images of a stranger in old photographs."

"That's real tough on a kid, I know. But, no."

Trace shook his head. "I can't count abandoning a family among my many sins. I'm footloose and fancy-free—and have been for many long years now."

"Not ever even been tempted to settle down?" Hallie queried lightly, hearing her earlier suspicions about him not being marriage material confirmed.

"Oh, once or twice, I suppose. But somehow things just never seemed to work out quite the way I hoped and planned. In the end, I was never the right man, or she was never the right woman, or it was simply never the right time or place."

"Hey, you two," Aunt Gwen called, interrupting their dialogue. "I thought you were ready to go. Are you just going to stand there gabbing all afternoon, or are you coming? I don't know about you, but I've been up since early this morning, so I could really do with some lunch right about now. I figured we could have the rest of that fried chicken and the cold salads I made for your supper last night, Hallie."

"That sounds wonderful, Aunt Gwen, and yes, we'll be right there," Hallie said. Then, turning back to Trace, she went on.

"Remind me when we go home to have you take a look at the power. There hasn't been any at the farmhouse since the thunderstorm last evening, and Aunt Gwen assures me it was never turned off after my grandmother died. She thinks maybe a fuse has been blown or something. I forgot to check it out myself earlier, and I'm not sure whether the house still has one of those old fuse boxes, either…you know, with the kind of fuses that have to be replaced by hand."

"Don't worry. I'll get it fixed first thing," Trace assured her.

Then, after Hallie had paid for her purchases, they returned to the car and headed toward Meadowsweet.

Chapter 8

Of Pickles and Pantries

On the way home Hallie thought she glimpsed the great black wolf racing amid the tall rows of corn once more. But because she could not be sure, she made no comment to either Aunt Gwen or Trace, not wishing to alarm the former and somehow certain the latter would only favor her with some insolent look or remark.

After all, it was not as though one ought not to expect to see wolves now and then around their namesake, Wolf Creek.

Still, normally, they were animals who ran in packs, so it was exceedingly rare to spy one on its own, without its mate, cubs or other companions. She wondered why it was alone. Given its obvious size and strength, she thought it was unlikely it had been driven from its pack, as young males who sought to challenge the dominant male generally were. So it must have left of its own accord.

Or perhaps, as anomalous as the idea seemed to her, it had never been part of a pack at all, had always been on its own—footloose and fancy-free.

As that thought occurred to her, Hallie glanced covertly from beneath her lashes at Trace, firmly ensconced in the driver's seat, his hands strong and sure upon the steering wheel. She still could not shake the notion that he and the wolf had too much in common, right down to their scarred left cheeks, for it to be mere coincidence.

But of course, it was simply ridiculous to assume they were somehow one and the same creature, that Trace was, in reality, a werewolf or something. In the bright light of the afternoon, Hallie realized how ludicrous that idea was, knew her imagination was running rampant again and must be reined in.

Still, what about all the vague snatches of scary

wolf stories she remembered from her youth? No, surely, they were nothing more than tales told to frighten misbehaving children—or dredged up to thrill young girls at slumber parties, like the one about the couple parked in the boondocks, kissing, who heard a news report on the radio about a violent, deranged escaped convict with a hook for a hand. Upset, the girl insisted on going home, and once there, she and her boyfriend discovered a hook on the handle of their car door, so they had known if they not driven away when they had, they would have fallen victim to the convict....

"Aunt Gwen," Hallie inquired, curious, once they had reached the farmhouse and begun putting away the groceries in the kitchen. "Do you know anything at all about the history of Wolf Creek?"

"No, not much, dear. Why do you ask?"

"Oh, no real reason. I suppose that seeing it again, I was just curious, that's all...you know, how it came to be founded, how it received its name, and so forth. I know there's a creek that runs through town and the farm, as well, and I imagine wolves and other animals used to come there to drink...probably still do...."

"I've heard the land on which Wolf Creek was

built was sacred to the American Indians," Trace announced, as he set the last of the grocery sacks on the kitchen counter. "Not because it was an ancient burial ground or anything like that, but because of the wolves themselves. Many peoples considered them sacred beasts, imbued with strange and mysterious powers, and connected them with Mother Moon—no doubt because they are notorious for howling at her."

"Yes, that's quite true." Aunt Gwen nodded sagely. "During our travels, my late husband and I came into contact with many ancient cultures who revered the wolf. Some even believed a great she-wolf was their universal mother."

"There are also tribes who think a great wolf was their universal father," Trace said. "For those who are sick, the wolf is a healer, and for those who are lost, a pathfinder. Whether for good or ill, to spy one is thought a powerful sign—for the wolf is elusive, and only a few chosen ones are favored by it. To see it in a vision quest is the most significant omen of all, for then it becomes one's totem animal, and one is always guided and protected by it.

"A spirit talker cloaked in a wolf skin is an undeniably fearsome sight, and there are those who say that a true shaman or witch can, by casting a powerful magic spell, actually bind a man to a wolf, making them one, because Man and Beast have always been inextricably linked since the beginning of Time. I've always thought the howl of a wolf is one of the few truly atavistic sounds left in this world, that it still stirs something primal in us all…" Trace paused for a moment. Then he spoke again, abruptly changing the subject. "Do either of you know where the breaker box is? I need to find out what's wrong with the power and fix it."

"Oh, yes, Trace." Crossing the checkerboard tile floor, the older woman opened the door to the pantry. "It's right inside here."

"Well, that's odd." Hallie frowned, puzzled. "I—I could have sworn it was someplace else in the house when I was a child, in a…in a closet in the main hall or somewhere. But perhaps I'm simply remembering wrong…."

"I don't know, dear," Aunt Gwen told her. "However, I do know that at one point, Hennie had the entire house rewired. The original electrical wiring had got very old, of course, and I believe it was becoming a fire hazard. So perhaps the box was moved during that process."

"Yes, if that's the case, you're no doubt right, Aunt Gwen. I know I was extremely surprised to find the kitchen looking the way it does now...so different from how it was originally."

"Is it? I'm afraid I wouldn't know anything about that, child, as this is how it's been ever since I came here. It's a cheerful kitchen, I've always thought...so white and bright and sunny. Even on the grayest of rainy days, the kitchen never seems nearly as dark and gloomy as the rest of this old farmhouse does."

"I suppose I'll get used to it in time." Hallie glanced around the kitchen—but in search of what, she did not know. "During my childhood, contrary to the way it is now, the kitchen used to be one of the darkest rooms in the house, with aged oak cabinets and a yellow pine floor. The bricks of the fireplace are actually red-brown beneath all that white paint.

"No matter how dreary it must have been in reality, I always found it quite cozy myself, and I used to imagine it was the kitchen inside some fairy-tale cottage—for, truly, that is what it looked like—and that Gram herself was some enchanting witch.

"There used to be a butcher block here, in the middle of the room, where she sorted the fresh herbs from her garden, tying them up into neat bunches before hanging them from an old rack above to dry.

"I can't…I just can't imagine why she changed it all, and it seems to me, as well, that there used to be something here that I've forgotten and that's not here now. But I don't know what it could be. But, then, of course, I was only a child at the time, so perhaps my memory is playing tricks on me." Hallie shrugged, smiling.

"Well, I hate to say it, dear, but speaking as one who spent most of her life cooking on a camp stove, I deeply appreciate a kitchen with all the modern amenities—and what you've described as its previous state, as enthralling as it might have appeared to you as a child, makes me believe Hennie had quite good reasons for updating it all. Why, it must have been positively depressing to work in before!"

"Now that you've put it that way, I guess it probably was, Aunt Gwen." Hallie laughed. "You'll have to forgive me. I'm afraid I've spent much more time in front of a computer than I ever have in a kitchen. Once I grew up and moved out of Aunts Agatha and Edith's town house, I tended to survive on pizzas delivered from the nearest parlor, Chinese takeout and sandwiches from the local deli."

"Good grief, Hallie." The elderly lady eyed her askance. "What a diet. Why, it's a miracle you don't weigh three hundred pounds from all that fast food!"

"Well, I confess I also spent a lot of time jogging to keep in shape. But I don't suppose that's going to be the most practical option here at Meadowsweet. I guess I thought there would still be horses to ride, the way there were during my childhood."

"Oh, no, child, there haven't been horses here at the farm for a long time now. They were gone even before I came here. Hennie said they'd got to be too much for her manage on her own, and young Tommy Adams, who used to help out around the place, had finally graduated from high school and gone off to college.

"After that, she couldn't find anybody else who wanted to work here. The other farmers around here all have their own places to tend to, and all these kids nowadays seem to be such couch potatoes—glued to their cell phones, MP3 players, TVs and video games. I guess they're afraid a bit of fresh air or manual labor might kill them!

"We're actually pretty darned lucky Trace was looking for work, and that Frank sent him over here to us, because we probably would have had a difficult time locating anyone else to come out here on a regular basis—no matter how much we might have been willing to pay."

Lowering her voice, highly conscious of the man's presence in the small pantry, Aunt Gwen continued.

"If you ask me, Hallie, we got a real bargain in Trace! Room and board and a hundred dollars a week? Why, that's just dirt cheap. He could charge three times as much and still hope to receive it around here."

"Well, for pity's sake, Aunt Gwen," Hallie whispered. "Don't tell him that! I mean, we don't want to be compelled to pay him any more than we have to. Meadowsweet needs a lot of repairs, and some of them are going to be extremely costly."

"Yes, I realize that. Hallie, I've never been one to pry, so I don't know how you're fixed financially. I just assumed Aggie and Edie had left you suitably well off. After all, I believe they had quite a bit of money put by, and they didn't have anybody else to leave it to—although I suppose they might have endowed any number of charitable institutions with it. They were very much into good works, I know, just the way Father was.

"Anyway, what I'm trying to tell you is that if you need help with the expenses, I'll be more than happy to assist you. Thanks to you, Meadowsweet is still my home now, and I've never been a freeloader, but always pulled my own weight."

"That's so sweet of you, Aunt Gwen. But in all honesty, I'm not poor," Hallie declared. "Although Aunts Agatha and Edith actually did leave a lot of their fortune to charity, there were still handsome bequests to me from each of them, and I've done very well for myself with my job, too. And of course, even though Gram didn't leave a great deal of money, she had paid off the mortgage on the farm over the years. So Meadowsweet itself is free and clear.

"So I don't think we need to worry about funds. I guess it's simply that it was inevitable that some of Aunt Agatha's frugal ways should rub off on me. So although I'm scarcely in the same penny-pinching league as she was, I'm not much of a spendthrift, either, and if there's a bargain to be had, I'm not going to be foolish enough to turn it down."

"Nor should you, dear," Aunt Gwen insisted firmly. "Now, why don't you help me set the table for lunch? Trace," she called, "how're you coming in there?"

"I'm nearly finished," he answered. "It's just a simple matter of testing all these breakers, to see which ones have blown and to reset them, making sure there isn't a bad switch or something else at fault. All the lightning last night probably struck a transformer some distance away, sending an electrical surge through the lines. I'll be done in a jiffy."

"Good. Hallie, I think there's a fresh jar of bread-and-butter pickles in there on the pantry shelves, and one of olives, too. Why don't you fetch them, and I'll make us a relish tray to eat with our lunch. Some deviled eggs would be nice, as well. I'll set the eggs to boiling. It won't take more than a few minutes to fix them."

Bustling around the kitchen, humming cheerfully to herself, the older woman busied herself with the preparations for lunch, while Hallie stepped into the pantry just off the kitchen. There she found Trace at work on the breaker box, the end of a small flashlight jammed into his mouth, so the beam illuminated his labor.

"Do you want me to hold that for you?" she asked.

"No," he got out between his clenched teeth. "Just try the light now and see if it works, please."

Instinctively, Hallie reached for the long thin cord that used to dangle from the lightbulb when she was a child, only to discover it was nowhere to be found.

Trace correctly interpreted her gesture and quickly set her straight.

"Your grandmother had the whole house rewired, remember? There's a switch on the wall now."

"Of course. I—I didn't realize at first."

Flicking it, Hallie was glad to see it resulted in the lightbulb coming on, flooding the small pantry with brightness. She had been a bit unnerved before, being in such close proximity to Trace in the darkness. It had reminded her of the feel of the hardness and strength of his broad chest when, to prevent her from tripping and falling in the gravel, he had so briefly clasped her to him in the parking lot of Lucy Bodine's bed-and-breakfast.

Hallie did not want to think about that and the emotions that fleeting moment had evoked in her. She told herself sternly that it was only natural she should be physically attracted to Trace, that, after all, he was without a doubt the handsomest man she had ever before seen.

It was as though there were some strange animal magnetism about him that was so strong, it was almost tangible. She had never before sensed such a powerful charisma in any other man, something so uncanny and earthy. It seemed to emanate like an aura from his very being.

Try as she might, she simply could not put it down to just his good looks or to his long, lean body, corded with muscle. In the past, she had known many handsome men with physiques honed to perfection by hours spent in the gym.

But as she thought about them now, Hallie knew they had all lacked some indefinable quality Trace possessed. When he moved, it was with a grace and suppleness that had nothing to do with hard physical training, but, rather, that was inborn—like that of a wolf, she mused, once more unsettled by the notion.

"Earth to Hallie. Earth to Hallie. Come in, please. Are you receiving?"

Abruptly jolted from her reverie, observing how Trace stared at her, his blue eyes gleaming and crinkling at the corners, his lips twisted into a teasing smile, she blushed furiously, her eyebrows knitting into a frown of annoyance.

"Loud and clear, Trace. Sorry. I was momentarily lost in the past," she lied, reaching for the jar of pickles she spied on one shelf. "It must have been quite an undertaking—rewiring this entire house, I mean. I was wondering what all was involved, whether any of the walls had to be ripped out, if that's why Gram had several of the rooms repapered...."

"Maybe—although wires can usually be pulled through the walls and between floors without tearing them out. Did you need something else?"

"Yes, that jar of olives, if you don't mind. I don't think this pantry was meant for two people."

"No, I don't suppose it was."

Still, he did not take the hint, as she had hoped, and exit the pantry, and she suffered the distinctly discomposing impression that she was shut up with some dangerous caged animal, which was prepared to spring upon her at any minute.

"I'll tell you what—you bring the olives when you're done in here, Trace. I need to help Aunt Gwen with our lunch," she said, swallowing hard, her heart beating way too fast in her breast.

Clutching the bread-and-butter pickles, she turned and practically ran from close confines of the pantry, thumping the jar down on the kitchen counter. Behind her, Hallie thought she heard Trace laughing softly, mockingly. But when she glanced irately in his direction, his dark visage was impassive, and she decided she must have been mistaken.

How she wished she could just fire the man— that she had never even hired him in the first place.

But how could she explain such an act—either to him or to Aunt Gwen?

If questioned, as she surely would be, Hallie

could not insist Trace had behaved badly, treated her disrespectfully or made unwelcome advances toward her. To the contrary, he had been nothing if not exceedingly gentlemanly and helpful, figuratively rolling up his sleeves and literally pitching right in with the work, assisting with Aunt Gwen's luggage and the groceries, and fixing the power immediately upon their return home from Wolf Creek.

She had no reason to get rid of him—none, except that he somehow reminded her of that damned great black wolf, and were she to give voice to that cause, Hallie knew she would only appear ridiculous, that Aunt Gwen would certainly wonder if she really *had* taken leave of her senses.

Further, she felt unshakably sure her great-aunt was fully informed and correct about the difficulty of finding employees willing to turn their hands to farm labor at Meadowsweet. It would hardly be wise to exchange Trace—who was obviously a smart, capable man—for some pimply-faced kid who did not even know one end of a pitchfork from the other.

No, whether she liked it or not, Hallie was stuck with the drifter.

She was simply going to have to accept that and make the best of the situation.

"Hallie, child, the way you're going at that stuffing for the deviled eggs, it's going to be nothing but mush in a minute," Aunt Gwen chided gently. "If I knew you better, I expect I'd think you were all riled up about something."

"No...no, it's nothing like that." Hallie spoke untruthfully, not daring to glance at Trace. "I've just got my mind on a million other things, that's all, and wasn't paying any attention to what I was doing."

"Well, here, why don't you let me finish that, and you peel the eggs, then?" the elderly lady suggested. "Do you prefer dill pickles or bread-and-butter ones in the stuffing? And do you like a dollop of mustard? I always think it adds a bit more flavor."

"Either kind of pickles is fine with me, Aunt Gwen, and that's a yes to the mustard, as well. I wouldn't turn down a sprinkling of paprika, either."

"That all works just fine for me, too," Trace agreed calmly, when the older woman looked inquisitively at him. "I've never been a particularly fussy eater, so I generally tend to enjoy whatever's put on my plate."

"That must have made your mother pretty happy," the older woman noted.

"I guess it would have, had she been alive. But

she and my dad both died young. Their car was struck head-on by a drunk driver. They were both killed instantly. I didn't have any other relatives, so I'm afraid I grew up in a series of foster homes on the Indian reservation where I lived then. My father was an American Indian…an Apache." He unwittingly confirmed Hallie's earlier speculation about his mixed ancestry.

"Oh, dear, I'm so sorry about your parents, Trace," Aunt Gwen said, her face filled with sympathy. "I wouldn't have made that remark about your mother if I'd known."

"No need to apologize. You had no way of knowing, and although I've certainly missed my parents over the years, I seldom grieve for them now. It all happened such a long time ago."

No wonder Trace was not a drunk, Hallie thought, remembering his list of qualifications for a job at Meadowsweet. No wonder he had so accurately surmised the point in her life at which she had arrived with her homecoming.

He had once been in such a place in his own life.

After that, she felt much more charitable toward him, and surreptitiously, she ensured he got the best pieces of fried chicken and the largest helpings of the accompanying salads.

All her earlier fanciful imaginings about him

seemed even more ridiculous now. In reality, for all his undeniable attractiveness, she decided that deep down inside, he was probably a very sad, lonely man—a drifter, just as he had said.

Nothing less, nothing more.

Chapter 9

Putting Down Roots

Following lunch, Hallie accompanied Trace to the tack room attached to the barn, to ensure it would provide suitable accommodation for him. Much to her dismay, however, she discovered it was a complete shambles, and she could not see how he intended to live there.

"I'm afraid Aunt Gwen and I made only the most cursory of inspections of the barn this morning. So I had no idea, really, what terrible shape the tack room is actually in."

"Not to fear," Trace insisted. "A bit of hard work this afternoon will go a long way toward setting it to rights."

"But…it doesn't even have a bed!"

"That's no problem. I've got a camp cot and a sleeping bag in my pickup truck, so I'll be quite comfortable until I can get a proper bed."

"But if I'm to provide room and board for your hire, surely, it should be I who supplies the bed," Hallie declared, then blushed as she realized the wholly unintentional double entendre contained in her words. Hastily, she continued. "If only I'd known, we could have bought a bed at the discount store today. I shall certainly see to it tomorrow."

Then, before any more could be said, murmuring about having chores of her own that needed tending, she excused herself and hurried from the tack room, feeling guilty and ashamed that she had not offered him a bedroom in the farmhouse.

There were four perfectly good large airy bedrooms upstairs—only two of which were now currently in use. Still, Hallie had hesitated to install Trace in one of the other two, one of which had belonged to her mother and the other of which had been Gram's. Like Hallie's own childhood bedroom, the former had remained untouched over the years, and of course, nothing had yet been done about the latter's, either.

Hallie suffered mixed feelings about both. Despite how much she had loved her mother and grandmother, she genuinely did not believe the rooms should be maintained as shrines to them. While she felt sure Gram must have had her own good reasons for leaving both her daughter's and granddaughter's rooms as they were, Hallie herself found the idea more than a little morbid and thought it had not been a healthy thing for her grandmother to have so preserved the past in such a fashion.

With that in mind, Hallie was determined to tackle her own bedroom, at least. For one thing, she was long through with the books, dolls, stuffed animals and other toys with which the shelves were littered. Had she returned as a child to Meadowsweet, she would have been glad to see them all. But now they were only a painful reminder to her of how she had been sent away back East, to embark upon a totally different life from the one she had envisioned when she had lived as a child at the farm.

So, armed with a box of large garbage bags she unearthed in the pantry, she headed upstairs, bent on conquering the childhood clutter.

Not even to herself did she admit she found the

idea of Trace being ensconced in one of the bedrooms at the farmhouse not only unnerving, but also secretly thrilling, so much so that she was inwardly relieved she had a reasonable excuse for not offering him one. Subconsciously, she feared that knowing he was just down the hall or, worse, right next door to her own bedroom would prove a temptation she did not want or need right now.

"What are you up to, child?" Aunt Gwen queried, exiting her own room, as Hallie reached the wide landing. "Surely there's not that much trash up here—although, in truth, I can't remember when the wastebaskets upstairs were last emptied."

"No, it's not that, Aunt Gwen. I simply thought I would have a go at cleaning my bedroom. Although I'll admit it does seem almost sacrilegious, given how Gram took such pains to preserve it, I'm no longer a child. Many of the room's contents look almost brand-new. I'm sure there are many deserving poor children who would enjoy having them. So I thought I would bundle all my old belongings up for the Salvation Army or Goodwill or whatever other charitable institutions Wolf Creek may possess."

"What a wonderful idea, child! I'll be happy to help you, if you like. I don't mean any disrespect toward Hennie, but I never did feel it was right to keep your and your mother's bedrooms looking like rooms in some museum. Still, I think it gave her some kind of comfort—for, on a dreary day, she used to sit in one or the other, lost in her memories. I was always very careful never to disturb her then—for I never wanted to intrude on her solitude, you know."

The elderly lady paused for a moment, remembering. Then she continued.

"Well, let us not waste another minute, Hallie! If we begin now, working together, we can get a great deal accomplished before bedtime—for I'm sure you do not want the room to be utter chaos when you retire this evening."

"No, not if I can avoid it, Aunt Gwen," Hallie agreed.

Companionably, the two women set to work, sorting through books and dolls, stuffed animals and toys, Hallie deciding which few she would keep for old time's sake, carefully tucked away in a chest somewhere, and what she would donate to charity.

The furniture itself was of good quality, being solid mahogany, and not the least bit childish. But the girlish canopy and matching comforter and dust ruffle were stripped from the double bed to be sacked up, as well. Much to Hallie's delight, a rummage through the large linen closet upstairs produced a much more sophisticated, hand-knotted, crocheted canopy, along with a beautiful, hand-stitched quilt and a delicate white eyelet dust ruffle.

"I'm so glad you have such an appreciation for these old things, Hallie," Aunt Gwen told her. "Many young women your age wouldn't, you know. They'd want something smart and modern, much more in keeping with the styles to be found at Ikea, rather than in an antiques store."

"I suppose that's one of the things Aunts Agatha and Edith managed to instill in me," Hallie explained. "To value the past and the treasured items handed down through successive generations. Aunts Agatha and Edith believed the fact that the world has become such a disposable society was utterly disgraceful, and that's something about which I firmly agreed with them. There's so much waste on our planet, it's pitiful."

With the beeswax Gram had always employed, Hallie and Aunt Gwen polished the bedroom furniture until it shone. They cleaned all the lamps and knickknacks, too, and washed the curtains and vacuumed the carpet.

Finally the room was finished, and although

they were both dirty and exhausted, they felt a deep sense of satisfaction as they gazed at their accomplishments, then at each other.

"Thank you so much for all your help, Aunt Gwen. I couldn't have done it without you!" Hallie said, giving the older woman a warm hug. "If you feel up to it tomorrow, we'll do Mom's room, too. There won't be nearly as much work involved with that, of course, because it's not crammed to bursting with childhood stuff."

"We'll need to do Hennie's room, as well, eventually." The elderly lady sighed. "I confess I'm not looking forward to that…so many memories for us both. But time marches on, and one way or another, those of us left behind have to get on with our lives as best we can. You remember that, dear, when my own time comes."

"Oh, Aunt Gwen, I hope that's not going to happen for a long time!" Hallie averred.

"Thank you, child. That's so sweet of you— and the truth is that I'm only seventy-three, and in great health, besides, thank the good Lord! So perhaps I'll live to be a hundred. You never know. Many people do nowadays. Well, I'm off to soak my tired old bones now and get cleaned up before supper. Don't try to manage all these bundles yourself, Hallie. Get Trace to help you."

"Oh, they're not that heavy."

"Maybe not. But the stairs in the main hall are rather steep, and...well, I just hate the thought of you going down them, carrying all these sacks. You might accidentally slip and fall...."

"Like Mom, you mean?" Hallie asked slowly, comprehension dawning. "Yes, I understand, Aunt Gwen. And I promise you, I don't want to break my neck on the stairs, the way Mom did. Not that she meant to fall, of course. It just... happened.

"I don't even remember it, you know. I don't know if I just wasn't there when it occurred, if I was outside playing or what, or if I've simply blocked the memory from my mind, because it was so shocking and ghastly a thing for a child to witness. Sometimes, I think I must have been present, and then, at others, I believe perhaps I only think I was.

"It's all such a jumble in my brain and so hard, after so many years, to separate what I actually saw or didn't see from what I was told over the years by Aunts Agatha and Edith and, more rarely, by Gram herself."

"I know, dear." The older woman patted Hallie's hand solicitously. "Childhood memories are frequently confusing that way. One hears a story so often that one comes mistakenly to believe one was actually there when the incident giving rise to the tale happened. I know there were things that occurred when Aggie and Edie were children, before I was even born, that I later came to think I'd had a part in, also. But that just wasn't true.

"So no doubt you *were* outside playing when your mother died. It was a bright summer's day, I understand, so that would have been only natural, wouldn't it?"

"Yes, you're right, of course." Hallie smiled tremulously. "I'm not even certain it was I who found her body... Sometimes, there's so much I wish I could remember about that day. But, then, at other times, I'm so grateful I can't recall much of anything about it. In the end, I don't know which is worse."

"Perhaps one day, when you're ready, it will all come back to you, Hallie—if that's what you truly want. In the meanwhile, you can take comfort from the fact that wherever Rowan and Hennie may be now, they're together again, just as they were in life."

"Yes, I'm glad of that. Well, don't use up all the hot water, Aunt Gwen! Even though I showered this morning, I'm unquestionably in need of a bath now. I don't remember when I last saw so much dust! Gram would have been so upset. She always kept the farmhouse spotless."

"That she did, dear. Well, I'm really off to the bathtub now. Don't forget to have Trace help you with those bundles."

"No, I won't. I promise."

Leaving the elderly lady to make her way down the hall to the main bathroom, Hallie headed downstairs and out to the tack room, where she discovered Trace had been equally as hard at work as she and Aunt Gwen had been in the bedroom.

"Good Lord. This doesn't even look like the same place." She gazed with astonishment at all he had managed to accomplish, the years of clutter, trash and dirt he had cleared out in a matter of hours.

All the old, rotten leather bridles and halters that had previously dangled from askew hooks in the walls were gone. Battered saddles astride rickety wooden racks had been got rid of, along with the racks themselves, moth-eaten blankets, torn rubber muck boots, long-rusted curry combs, ancient shoeing equipment, and cartloads of other accouterments previously used to maintain the horses once housed in the barn.

The tack room itself had been hosed down and swept clean, and in one corner Trace had erected his camp cot and unrolled his sleeping bag on top. He had set up a small camp table, too, on which he had placed an electric lantern.

"As I assured you, I'll manage just fine out here," he told her, tossing aside the rag he had been using to dry his wet hands. Plainly, he had washed up himself with the hose, as well. "Tomorrow I'll get started on the barn itself. Your great-aunt said something about you maybe wanting horses here at Meadowsweet again."

"I hadn't really given that a whole lot of thought yet," Hallie confessed. "Still, it would be nice—and great exercise, too."

"Not to mention practical, if you're intending actually to run this place as a farm again. From what Frank Kincaid told me, I don't believe your grandmother had done so in that regard for years, letting the land lie fallow instead."

"I think she had a hard time getting help," Hallie explained. "Naturally, people with their own farms work those and don't have time for anybody else's, and from what my great-aunt has said, it seems the kids hereabouts nowadays are more interested in electronic pursuits than in turning their hands to the land. Small farms like

Meadowsweet are a dying breed. It's just too difficult to compete with the giant farming corporations anymore."

"Why didn't your grandmother just sell the place, then?"

"She loved the land—she always said it was the only thing that endured—and she actually did have a small but thriving enterprise here, with chickens, her bees and her herb garden. She sold eggs, honey and other bee products, and dried herbs, locally—at the farmers' market on Saturdays, mostly. But I gather from Aunt Gwen that the two of them had ambitions about trying to expand, mainly by setting up a Web site and starting a mail-order business."

"With the right products, keywords and marketing, that's something that could prove highly successful," Trace mused aloud.

"Yes, I know. It's what I actually do for a living. I'm a graphic designer."

"Then you shouldn't have much trouble at all, implementing your grandmother and great-aunt's plan."

"No. I'm just not sure I want to sell bee pollen the rest of my days—or even if I'm going to stay here at the farm long term," she confided. "I do have a life back East—and a good job from which

I've taken a sabbatical. Right now, I'm just trying to get myself sorted out. I'm—I'm recently divorced...no children, thank goodness. Still, I didn't plan on a failed marriage.

"Anyway, that's one of the reasons why I'm not all that eager to leap headfirst into another relationship right off the bat—and why I haven't made up my mind yet about Meadowsweet's future, either. And although I'm very glad my great-aunt's here, her presence *has* complicated matters. If I wind up selling the farm, she'll be homeless, and somehow, I have the distinct impression she wouldn't be too keen on the idea of accompanying me back East, that she isn't any more interested in big-city living than you are, Trace."

"A body could do a lot worse than to settle down on this old farm," he pointed out. "It's got a great deal of potential. In fact, I've been saving all my life for a place just like this one. So if you decide to sell, I hope I'll be the first person you tell—because if the price is right, I'd be real tempted to make you an offer."

"I thought you were a drifter—footloose and fancy-free."

"I am. But there comes a time in every man's life when he comes to a fork in the road, and he's got to make a decision about which one to take. I reckon I'm about there now—and I never planned to be a drifter all my life. Your grandmother's old farmhouse is truly an outstanding piece of Victorian architecture, just the sort of rambling place filled with nooks and crannies, which I've always found interesting. I don't want to live in one of these modern boxes people are crammed into nowadays, in some neighborhood where all the houses look just alike and are jammed up next to one another like sardines in a can, and where there's a home owners' association with a whole bunch of rules to adhere to, neither. That wouldn't suit me at all."

"No, I don't suppose it would. All right, then. If I decide not to stay at Meadowsweet permanently, you'll be the first to know.

"Now, if you're not too worn out, would you mind giving me a hand upstairs in the house? I've got several sacks full of childhood stuff I'm getting rid of, and Aunt Gwen doesn't want me carrying them down the stairs in the main hall. The bundles aren't that heavy, but she's worried I'll trip and fall and break my neck on the stairs.

"That's how my mom died, right here at this very house, so I really don't want Aunt Gwen upset that I'm going to suffer a like fate."

"No problem. I'm sorry to hear that about your mother. That must have been rough—having your dad run off, then losing your mother."

"No harder than you losing your own parents because of a drunk driver, I don't guess. At least I had relatives who took me in, my grandmother's sisters, Aunts Agatha and Edith. I'm still not sure why Gram sent me away back East to them, but, anyway, that's what she did."

"Maybe she thought it would be too painful for you to grow up in the house where your mother died."

"Maybe. I don't know. But it's all water under the bridge now."

After walking with her back to the farmhouse, Trace carried all her neatly wrapped childhood belongings down to her Mini, loading them into the cargo space for delivery to the Salvation Army in the morning.

By then, Aunt Gwen was finished in the bathroom, and gratefully, Hallie filled the bathtub to indulge in her own long, hot soak. After that, the three of them ate supper, then played a couple of rounds of cards together in the back parlor.

But by ten o'clock, Hallie was so exhausted from yet another long day that she could scarcely keep her eyes open, and making her apologies to Aunt Gwen and Trace, she trudged upstairs to go to bed.

Moments later, after stripping off her clothes and donning a clean, fresh nightgown she had earlier unpacked from her luggage, she was fast asleep in her newly made bed.

Chapter 10

Only Bad Dreams

Despite her weariness, it was an uneasy, restless slumber into which Hallie slipped, and at some point she began to experience a vaguely disturbing dream that gradually metamorphosed into a dark, erotic nightmare.

She dreamed that despite all her and Aunt Gwen's hard work that afternoon, her childhood bedroom somehow mysteriously restored itself to its previous state of being, with all her books and dolls, stuffed animals and toys haphazardly cached upon the shelves.

Sometime in the night, one of the male dolls—dressed as an American Indian warrior and which Gram had once bought for her on some long-ago farmers' market day—began to argue with one of the stuffed animals, a wolf that was one of the few tourists' souvenirs that could be purchased in the small town of Wolf Creek.

As the two toys quarreled, they started some kind of a ritual pagan dance that mimicked a hunt, with the warrior brandishing his spear fiercely and the wolf cunningly dodging this way and that, so he eluded the deadly weapon at every turn.

To the increasingly louder tattoo of the drums that beat and echoed from somewhere in the shadows, the two toys ran and whirled and leaped across the shelves before suddenly bounding to the floor, where the carpet appeared eerily to have turned into a grassy meadow.

At first, recognizing she was asleep and dreaming, Hallie was only bemused by the antics of the warrior doll and the stuffed wolf, wondering why she should imagine such a bizarre but harmless event.

But then, slowly, as she watched from the bed where she lay dreaming, the tenor of the dance began to change, to take on a much more ominous tone, and much to her sudden horror, the two toys started to grow until they became full-sized replicas of their real-life counterparts—and then, right before her stricken gaze, they abruptly came alive.

Locked in the throes of their lethal dance, they spun faster and faster, until they began to merge somehow into one being. When the transformation was complete, the pounding of the drums abruptly ceased, and after a moment, moving silently on padded feet, the thing they had become came to stand beside her bed, looming over her in the darkness.

Hallie did not know if she was still asleep and dreaming, then, or if she had awakened. She knew only that her eyelids had fluttered open, and that by the dim, silvery glow of the moonlight that streamed through the sheer, gauzy folds of the freshly laundered curtains, she could see it was neither man nor beast who towered over her, but somehow both.

The terrifying creature's silky, shiny head boasted the upper face of an immense wolf, the largest she had ever seen, and just like that of the animal that had blocked her path last night, the black fur around its visage faded into silver-gray wisps, and a thin, jagged scar marred its left cheek. Its gleaming, predatory eyes appeared midnight blue in color in the half light, and its muzzle blended so smoothly with the lower half of a man's dark and heavily stubbled countenance that the two images seemed somehow as one.

The man-beast's front legs were those of a wolf, as well, with huge paws as big as a man's hands and tipped with sharp, hard black claws that looked capable of rending her from limb to limb. But the creature stood upright rather than on all fours, sporting the tall, powerful body and large heavy sex of a man.

Naked and rippling with muscle, he was so dark and hirsute that his broad chest matted with velvety black hair flowed into the glossy black pelt of his arms and shoulders and face, making it difficult to distinguish where man ended and beast began. Or perhaps they both were one and the same, Hallie thought numbly as she stared up at him, morbidly fascinated despite the sheer terror engendered in her by the creature.

Although his beautiful, full, bushy black tail that brushed the carpet-cum-grass was clearly discernible, his great hind legs seemed to be those a man one moment and those of a wolf the next, indeterminate, like the rest of him, confusing her, making her doubt what her wide green eyes truly beheld.

Surely the man-beast was something to be found only in a nightmare, dredged from the darkest, most secretive chasms of her subconscious— frightening, dangerous and magnificent, exuding fatal animal magnetism and menace, treacherously carnal and seductive, a throwback to some atavistic time, some primeval place of mystery and magic that humankind had finally and forever lost with the onslaught of progress and civilization.

So the shamans and witches of ancient cultures must have looked, Hallie realized in some dark cranny of her cloudy brain, when, cloaked in their animal skins, they had become the mythic shapeshifters who had given rise to the stories of werewolves and other only half-human beings that had peopled the tales of yore, subtly taking on the appearance and characteristics of the beasts they had portrayed, seeming to metamorphose into the actual creatures themselves.

For a long, apprehensive moment in her dream, the man-beast did nothing but gaze down at her silently, rapaciously, his fierce blue eyes hypnotizing her, paralyzing her, as those of a predator rivet its prey a heartbeat before the stronger closed in to kill the weaker.

Survival of the fittest. That was the law of the jungle—and Hallie had never been more conscious of it than in that instant when, without warning, snarling low in his throat, he suddenly sprang upon her, abruptly releasing her from his peculiarly mesmerizing spell.

Wholly horrified then, driven by pure survival instinct, Hallie screamed and then screamed again as the creature pounced upon her, his harsh breath hot against her throat, his mighty arms and legs caging her in on both sides as he crouched over her shrinking figure. But in her dream, no one at Meadowsweet heard her panicked shrieks, or if they did, they ignored them. Or maybe she only thought she screamed and, in reality, made no sound at all, as is the way of a nightmare.

Desperately, determinedly, she tried at first to escape and then, when that failed, to fight the wolfish man-beast, to defend herself against him. But much to her consternation, Hallie discovered she was oddly dazed and lethargic, as though she were ill or drunk or drugged.

She seemed to move as though she were somehow trapped in a slow-motion segment in a John Woo movie, as though her mind no longer had any control over her body. She could not free herself. Her resolute but ultimately pitiful attempt to battle the creature was futile. She was easily overcome when he captured her wrists in a tight grip and dragged them beneath her, pinning them with one strong paw.

As he did so, he forced her supple back to arch in unwitting invitation, her full round breasts to strain upward, her taut nipples to quiver with inadvertent enticement against his massive chest, her hips to thrust alluringly against his own, her downy womanhood to skim his potent sex, greatly exciting them both.

Hallie shivered with both terror and shame at the involuntary, quickening, melting response she experienced in response to the man-beast. Surely, there was something terribly wrong with her to feel such unnatural arousal at the sight of the creature, to yearn to couple with it, despite her fear.

She felt sickened and mortified by her desire. But she could not escape from it, any more than she could flee from the man-beast. She thought she must be but a heartbeat from death—or worse. Her blood thrummed so fiercely in her veins that it was as though the wild, primal drumbeat that had somehow conjured the creature into existence pounded inside her, setting her to throbbing and aching for release.

Whimpering helplessly, Hallie thrashed her giddy head, instinctively exposing her long white throat, baring its soft pale vulnerability to the man-beast, in an age-old gesture of appeasement and submission. She expected he would rip out her jugular vein, causing her blood to spew in a mortal torrent from her body.

But when he at last lowered his dusky, undeniably proud, handsome head, it was to give her a long, languorous lick instead, his rough, inciting tongue following the graceful arch of her throat from its tiny hollow upward to her chin. Despite her dread, Hallie felt a sudden wild perverse thrill of anticipation and excitement shudder through her entire body, and she wanted to die.

Sensing that, the man-beast dew back slightly so he could see her ashen face, his glimmering eyes boring down into hers, smoldering with a dark and dangerous hunger that made her breath catch on a ragged sob as she recognized his passionate, depraved intent.

He wanted her—and he meant to have her.

Once more, Hallie struggled mightily but vainly to gather her wits, to twist violently free from him, to escape from him. But much to her dismay, he subjugated her totally. Dizzy and weak, she was completely powerless against his immense strength as he pressed her down into the soft plump mattress upon which she lay.

Still holding her prisoner with one paw, he began with the other to explore her, searching and mapping every curve and hollow of her vital young body, which had been wakened by other lovers in the past and was now eager and unsated from her current self-imposed abstinence.

She felt the creature's fervid breath against her ear and upon her heated skin as he sniffed and nibbled her, seeming more beast than man as his muzzle and mouth, his teeth and free paw roamed over her. Gently, he nuzzled her earlobe, his long pink tongue trailing languidly across her cheek and down her neck to her burgeoning breasts.

Deeply, he inhaled the sweet wild fragrance of her, and in response, Hallie could smell the feral forest scent of him increasing, growing ever stronger and muskier, maddening her own senses, however unwillingly she acquiesced to them.

Finding the highly sensitive place on one shoulder where it joined her nape, the creature bit her tenderly, his tongue flicking deliberately against her skin, causing another tremulous shiver to course through her violently. Obliviously, she cried out against him, a low, animalistic moan Hallie was only dully aware came from her own throat.

She could not believe this was happening, that it was real.

But, no, she reminded herself, it was not. It was only a strange, horrible dream—a nightmare, however utterly fantastic, frightening and fervent she might find it.

Still, no matter how hard she tried, Hallie could not seem to waken herself from it from it, to drive the man-beast from her sleeping thoughts. In slumber, her fanciful imagination was now fully unleashed, running rampant with visions and desires she had not known she possessed, that shocked and shamed her to the very core of her being.

Never before had she experienced such a graphically sexual and bestial dream, in which all her senses appeared to have come to the fore, to be quick with a life and a will all their own, separate and apart from the dictates of her own consciousness. She seemed to have no mind of her own, no ability or will left with which to contest against the creature.

It was though as her brain had shut down, as though all her bones had turned molten inside her, leaving her as weak and limp as a rag doll, so the creature might do as he pleased with her, turning her this way and that, poking and prodding into every single nook and cranny of her being.

As her concupiscent dream continued to unfold in her mind, Hallie's childhood bedroom gradually evanesced into mist, to be replaced by an ancient, long-shadowed forest wherein she and the man-beast lay upon sweet wild grass crushed and trampled to release its green perfume. She seemed to watch from someplace far above as his mouth covered hers, his tongue plunging deep and insistent between her lips.

She wanted to protest the invasion, but, instead, she felt her mouth opening and yielding to him, her tongue meeting his ardently, silently urging him on. She could feel his sharp canine teeth upon her soft, pliant lips, caressing and biting. And then his unstill mouth and tongue, his teeth and free paw seemed to be everywhere upon her, kissing and licking, nipping and petting, heightening her dismaying but irrefutable desire and deepening her humiliation that she should be so inexorably and provocatively stimulated by him.

In some dim corner of her mind, Hallie prayed the creature would quickly finish with her. But much to her distress, he was not so inclined, fondling her breasts until they ached with passion, her nipples taut and trembling beneath his teasing tongue.

His sleek, corded muscles bunching and quivering sinuously, the man-beast wrapped himself around her, growling and panting as he continued his exploration of her body, growing ever more excited as she unwittingly bucked and writhed against him. Despite that they were sharp and hard, the creature's claws felt like rough raw silk as he dragged them lightly down her firm but soft belly and along the insides of her quavering thighs, causing an electric shock to surge from her fingertips to her toes.

The strong, musky smell of him mingled with her own scent, intoxicating them both, and when, ensnaring his paw in her now-tangled blond hair, he lifted her head to press it against his sweat-dampened chest, Hallie could taste the thin layer of salt that encrusted his fleecy flesh, adding pungent spice to the musk. She knew her own skin was equally sheeny with perspiration and that it tasted salty, too, upon his own tongue.

Time passed. Hallie had no idea how much, although in her dream, it seemed an eternity in which she drifted, dazed and throbbing vividly in every part of her, lusting for the man-beast to take her, to provide release for what he had so expertly and tightly wound within her—so skillfully and savagely inciting her that she felt she had actually become an animal herself, a she-wolf in season, ready and frantic to be mated.

Still, endlessly, it seemed, the creature tormented her, scattering her senses to the four winds that soughed through the amorphous, atavistic forest wherein they twined, leaving her faint and breathless, floating in a dark, timeless place above the fragrant green grass that was their soft mating bed. Mingled sweat bathed their bodies, glistening in the moonlight that filtered through the filmy canopy formed by the leafy branches of the trees above.

Fear and the perverse, perilous excitement that shocked and horrified her continued to fill Hallie's being, stoking the fire that burned in her blood, its flames fed still further as the man-beast slid down her body, his hard sex a portentous threat, a bewitching promise as his hot mouth scalded her belly and thighs.

Then, mercilessly, he opened her, bent his head to taste her, his tongue dipping deep into the mellifluous dark blond heart of her.

Time and again, the brazen creature lapped her, parting her swollen nether lips to spread her sweet-flowing moisture lingeringly along the soft folds and crevices that trembled beneath his touch, and around the little nub that was the key to her delight, that quickened and quivered as he teased and taunted it, until she was like a wild thing beneath him, desperately craving release.

At long last, suddenly releasing her pinioned hands and turning her over so her face was pressed into the pillow, his paws lifting her hips into position to receive him, the man-beast spread her eagerly yielding thighs wide and mounted her urgently, his need now as great as her own.

Hard and deep, he drove into the warm, willing channel of her womanhood, his sex filling her with welcome fullness and pleasure. Her hands clawing the sheets on the bed, Hallie goaded him on with her low, hoarse moans of desire and delight, crying out as, his paws digging bruisingly into her hips, he thrust into her faster and faster, his breath coming in harsh, heated rasps in the moonlit darkness.

Her violent climax seized her swiftly and savagely, erupting inside her in a flood of blinding sensation that left her gasping for air and shuddering uncontrollably in its aftermath, waves of ecstasy pulsing like stormy breakers through her body. The creature's own release came just as quickly and explosively as hers, as with a fierce, triumphant howl, he spilled himself inside her, crushing her hips against him brutally until, finally, he was sated.

Chapter 11

The Face at the Window

Still gasping for breath, Hallie started violently, wide-awake from her disturbingly sexual dream, abruptly sitting straight up in bed, her heart pounding furiously in her breast.

For a moment, drowsy and disoriented, she did not know where she was, and she mistakenly believed she had somehow been ominously transported from her bedroom to a long-shadowed forest somewhere far beyond this earthly realm.

The aftermath of the powerful climax she had

experienced in her dream, her nightmare of the man-beast, still held her in its grip, its aftershocks continuing to course through her body before gradually ebbing and subsiding.

She was terrified to glance at the pillow beside her, half afraid the bizarre, half-human creature her subconscious mind had conjured still lay beside her in the bed, as though she had somehow actually dreamed him into a real existence.

At that horrifying thought, Hallie briefly covered her face with her hands, then dragged them roughly through her unkempt blond hair.

It was only a dream—a god-awful nightmare, she reassured herself firmly.

Desperately she wished she had never quit smoking. She could have used a cigarette right now, to steady her nerves—or a good stiff drink. Still, there was probably nothing stronger than elderberry wine in the entire farmhouse.

Gram had never drunk much, and she had been almost as bad as Aunts Agatha and Edith in her condemnation of strong liquor. A lack of fondness for hard alcohol appeared to be one of the few things on which all the sisters had seen eye to eye.

Trace would most certainly have a cigarette, Hallie knew. Still, the notion of venturing outside in her nightgown and bare feet to the tack room at this late hour, to inform him she needed a smoke, would surely only make him think that was nothing more than a pretext and that she had other ideas entirely.

Looking at the alarm clock on the nightstand, she saw it was nearly three. No, she could not go out there at this hour. Even if she were desperate and did not care in the least what he thought, the man had worked hard all day. Common courtesy alone dictated that she not interrupt his own slumber, just because a nightmare had disturbed hers.

Further, now that she thought about it, Hallie irrationally blamed Trace for the whole bad dream. After all, it was he who, earlier that afternoon, during his dialogue with Aunt Gwen, had put the image of a spirit talker cloaked in a wolf skin into Hallie's head, thereby no doubt triggering her nightmare.

Even if there were nothing more than elderberry wine in the house, she really could do with a drink to settle herself down so she could get back to sleep, Hallie decided at last, reaching for her robe, which lay at the foot of the bed, just as its childhood counterpart had always done. Shrugging it on, she tossed back the covers and swung her feet over the side of the bed—freezing in fear when she suddenly spied a hideously distorted reddish white face, like that of a devil, peering in at her through one of the bedroom windows.

A long, loud scream tore from her throat, and abruptly galvanized into action, Hallie bolted from the room, yelling frantically for Aunt Gwen.

"Hallie! Hallie, what is it, dear? What's wrong?" The elderly lady came scurrying from her own bedroom, flicking on lights and clearly alarmed.

"Oh, my God, Aunt Gwen! There's a—a *monster* at my bedroom window!"

"A—a *monster!* Oh, Hallie, child, surely it was only a bad dream!"

"No, no, it was a monster. I saw it, I tell you! Oh, God, we've got to get Trace...call the sheriff's department. Is there a gun in the house?"

"There are...there are rifles and shotguns in the gun case downstairs. But if you're talking about a handgun, no, Hennie never kept anything like that around here."

Just then, as the two women stood clutching each other in the upstairs hall, a sharp, short bark followed by a low, vicious growling reached their ears, and then there was sound of someone or some*thing* crying out and footsteps pounding along the upstairs verandah outside.

"There! What did I tell you! Call the sheriff, Aunt Gwen! I'll fetch Trace!"

"No, don't you dare go outside, Hallie! We don't know who—or what—may be out there. Why, if—if you ask me, it doesn't even sound human!"

"I can't just leave Trace alone out there in the tack room. Whatever's out there might attack him!"

Without further ado, Hallie raced downstairs to the library, to where the gun case stood against one wall. Much to her relief, a frantic rummage through her grandmother's desk produced what she hoped was the right key, and with trembling fingers, she inserted it into the lock. Once she had got the glass door open, she jerked out an old-fashioned, double-barreled shotgun, then realized she had not a clue as to how to load it.

Praying it already contained shells, she ran to the kitchen's back door and, after peering through its window to be certain there was no one about, unbolted it and flung it open wide.

"Trace!" she shouted at the top of her lungs. "Trace!"

"It's me, Hallie. I'm here." He spoke softly, startling her horribly by suddenly materializing like a wraith from the shadows, barefoot and naked to the waist, revealing a muscular chest matted with fine black hair, reminding her uneasily of the man-beast in her dream. "Is that gun loaded?" he asked.

"Yes…no…I don't know," she gasped out, trying to catch her breath. "What—what are you doing here, Trace? Why aren't you in the tack room?"

"I'm a light sleeper, and when I heard all the ruckus, I got up to investigate. Get back inside the house." Expertly, it seemed to her, he broke open the shotgun. "It's empty. Where are the shells?"

"In the gun case in the library."

"Get them, while I keep watch. Hurry, Hallie!"

Quickly, she pelted back to the library and, from the bottom of the gun case, grabbed an open box of what she hoped were the right shells. Much to her relief, when she returned to the back door, Trace accepted them without question, deftly loading two of them into the shotgun, then snapping shut the breech.

"Lock the door behind me," he ordered, "and don't open up again unless it's me or the law outside. Do you understand?"

Hallie nodded, swallowing hard.

"I won't. Trace…be careful."

"Don't worry about me. Just keep yourself and Mrs. Lassiter safe." Then, without another word, he headed into the moonlit darkness.

As Hallie watched him disappear, she was

eerily struck by how much he seemed to have metamorphosed into a wolf in that moment, running with his body bent low, his long, shaggy hair streaming back in the wind. It appeared almost as though he were no longer human, and his words to her earlier about a true shaman or witch being able to bind a man and a wolf as one suddenly returned to haunt her.

What did she know about Trace, really?

Shivering a little, Hallie closed and bolted the door, nearly jumping out of her skin when Aunt Gwen suddenly appeared in the kitchen.

"Oh, dear, I'm so sorry. I didn't mean to startle you, child," the older woman said. "I've phoned for Sheriff O'Mackey, and he's on his way here. I take it that was Trace at the door, that you managed to wake him. My goodness, I hope he's not gone out there unarmed!"

"No, he had one of the shotguns from Gram's gun case—and he certainly seemed to know how to use it, too."

"Trace is a man of many talents, I suspect. Why don't I make us a cup of hot tea, Hallie? I always find that so soothing."

"You have one if you like, Aunt Gwen. To be honest, what I could really use right now is a drink."

"Well, dear, as you probably know, nobody in the

Dewhurst family has ever held with hard liquor—and that included Hennie. However, I do know she kept a bottle of apricot brandy around here somewhere, which she would occasionally have a sip of after supper. Yes, here it is," Aunt Gwen announced triumphantly, as she pulled the bottle and two snifters from one of the kitchen cabinets.

After pouring the brandy into the glasses, she handed one to Hallie.

"Drink up, child. I'm sure you're right, and that it will help to steady our nerves. I just hope Sheriff O'Mackey doesn't smell the alcohol on our breath and assume we were hitting the bottle and imagined this entire dreadful episode. Now, tell me about the...the monster, as you called it, that you saw at your bedroom window, Hallie. What did it look like?"

"Ghastly...just absolutely ghastly, Aunt Gwen! I've—I've never before seen anything so hideous in my entire life. That's—that's why I thought it was a monster. It just—just didn't seem human...all distorted and, and somehow crumpled, an awful shade of red and white, like a...a demon or something."

"Oh, dear, after I'd had a brief chance to calm down a little and think, I thought perhaps that's what it was. Rest assured, it was no monster, child, but a real human being, however abominable in appearance he seemed.

"You see, I think it was Scarecrow you saw—although why he was peering into your bedroom window, especially at this wee hour, I simply can't imagine. But, then, he's really not all there in the head, so maybe he's finally gone completely off the deep end."

"Scarecrow?"

"Yes, unfortunately, however cruel it may sound, that's what everybody calls him—although not out of any desire to hurt him, I hasten to assure you, but because that's the name he gives himself when asked. I don't believe anyone knows his real name, not even he himself.

"He was badly burned, you see, in a terrible fire at a warehouse sometime before he moved to Wolf Creek. It left him grossly disfigured, his face all twisted, one eye askew, and, yes, his skin badly crumpled, as you said, from all the grafts that were necessary to save his life. It's truly a miracle he even survived.

"Anyway, nobody's ever been able to identify him properly, because none of us knows where he came from. He just showed up in Wolf Creek one day, a very long time ago, Hennie told me once—in fact, if I recall right, it was shortly after you went to live with Aggie and Edie during your childhood. And if his fingerprints are in any law-enforcement database, they're useless now. His hands were burned, too, and are awfully scarred."

"I see. Well, naturally, I'm very sorry for the man. Still, Aunt Gwen, he's a Peeping Tom, at the very least, and quite possibly even dangerous!"

"Hallie, I know it seems like that to you at the moment, and I don't blame you for feeling that way, either. But in all honesty, Scarecrow has never hurt a single soul in town, and I've never heard any reports about him being a Peeping Tom, either. I simply can't imagine what possessed the man to clamber up to the upstairs verandah and peer inside your bedroom window."

"Well, maybe he's finally flipped—just as you said."

There was no time for further conversation, because by then, Sheriff Ned O'Mackey had arrived, the red and blue lights on his patrol car flashing brightly in the front yard as he pulled up on the circular gravel drive.

Trace greeted him out front, briefly explaining the situation. Then he and the sheriff came into the house, so Hallie could make a full report.

"It sure sounds like old Scarecrow," the sheriff agreed slowly, chewing on the end of the pencil with which he was making copious notes on a small, spiral-bound pad. "I don't know what came over him, Ms. Muldoon. Maybe he's gone clean off his nut at last, like your great-aunt suggested, or maybe he just got liquored up and took a wild notion to have a gander at you.

"I mean, you're newly returned to Wolf Creek, ma'am, and you're the spitting image of your mama, besides. I always thought she was one of the prettiest gals in town when she and I were growing up. It's a real shame she died so young.

"Anyway, if it's all right with you two ladies, Trace here's going to take me upstairs to have a look at the verandah. I understand there was some sort of a fracas up there…that Scarecrow was attacked by a vicious dog or something during his Peeping-Tom activities. You got any dogs on this farm, Ms. Muldoon?"

"No, Sheriff," Aunt Gwen answered, at her great-niece's inquiring glance. "After the last one died, Hennie told me she wasn't going to get another, that she was too old to be taking care of a hound dog anymore, and she couldn't abide those little frou-frou pedigreed mutts so many elderly ladies seem to have these days.

"So I'm afraid all we've got here at Meadowsweet is an old tomcat, who's way too sassy and independent for his own good…comes and goes just as he pleases. I haven't even seen him for a couple of days now."

"I—I think maybe it…maybe it was a wolf that attacked Scarcecrow," Hallie said hesitantly. "Possibly even a rabid one."

"What on earth would make you think that, ma'am?" the sheriff asked, a puzzled frown knitting his brow.

At some length, hoping she did not sound as though she were as crazy as Scarecrow appeared to be, Hallie explained what had happened the previous evening, how the huge black wolf had run out in front of her car, then leaped on its hood.

"I was going to tell Aunt Gwen about it, but…what with trying to get settled in and all, I just forgot, and I didn't really want to discuss the matter with anybody else, Sheriff, because I'm well aware how wildly improbable it sounds. Still, it *did* happen, and if the wolf *is* rabid and has bitten this man, Scarecrow, then he needs immediate medical treatment."

"Yes, you're certainly right about that. I'll issue a bulletin and get some officers out right away to search for him. He lives in a little shack up the road a piece, and that's probably where he's gone. I don't believe he'll have run away or anything like that." Folding up his notepad, Sheriff O'Mackey turned to Trace. "You want to show me that verandah now, son?"

"Yes, sir. We can go back outside and up the external stairs. Then we won't have to traipse through Ms. Muldoon's bedroom."

"That'd be fine. Lead the way."

Once the sheriff had finished inspecting the verandah, then got back into his patrol car and, after yakking briefly on his radio, driven slowly away, Trace returned to the farmhouse to ensure that Hallie and her great-aunt were all right.

"You're one of the chosen ones, you know, Hallie," he told her after Aunt Gwen had bidden them both good-night and gone back upstairs to bed. "Otherwise, you would never have seen that great black wolf, and he wouldn't have appointed himself as your protector...wouldn't have been keeping an eye on Meadowsweet nor gone after Scarecrow, either. It's rare for wolves to attack people. He must have thought the old lunatic intended you some kind of harm."

Hallie shuddered visibly at the thought.

"Why would this man, Scarecrow, want to hurt me?" she wondered aloud. "I've never done anything to him. I don't even know him."

"I don't know." Trace shook his head. "Maybe

he didn't. Maybe he only wanted to get a look at you, just as the sheriff said. You *are* a very attractive woman, Hallie. I noticed it right off, when you opened the front door this morning," he declared, smiling at her.

"I wish you'd keep those kind of thoughts to yourself!" she hissed, annoyed—although if she were honest with herself, she knew she would admit she was secretly pleased he appreciated her blond good looks.

"Honestly, Trace! I've just had two of the worst days of my entire life, and the topper was having to tell the local sheriff about that wolf's bizarre behavior. It'll probably be all over town tomorrow that I'm as loony as Scarecrow! And you just stand there, flirting with me.

"Why is it that every single man alive believes every problem around can be solved by a quick roll in the hay?"

"They don't. They just think they'll feel a whole lot better about their problems afterward!" he insisted, now grinning at her impudently.

"Where's that shotgun?" Hallie queried, wondering if it were him or the snifter of apricot brandy that had gone to her head.

"Back in the gun case. You don't actually think I'd be fool enough to stand here teasing a spitfire like you if I thought you had a shotgun handy, do you?"

"Good night, Mr. Coltrane!"

"Good night, Ms. Muldoon. Sweet dreams."

Chapter 12

Settling In

Climbing the staircase in the main hall to her bedroom, Hallie thought she would probably not get another wink of sleep that night. The disturbingly erotic dream that had haunted her earlier, capped off by seeing the poor disfigured lunatic, Scarecrow, at her window, would surely keep her wide-awake, tossing and turning restlessly.

But in the end, whether it was the warmth of the brandy or of Trace's smile, once she was again safely in her bed, she found her eyelids growing heavy, and without even realizing it, she slipped into slumber within minutes, eventually sleeping so deeply that the following morning, she did not awaken until noon.

Even then, she might have continued abed, had not a gentle rap on her door been followed by Aunt Gwen and, trailing close in her wake, Trace bearing a breakfast tray.

"Rise and shine, Sleeping Beauty," he greeted her, smiling lazily at her. "The day's a-wastin', and there are cows to be milked and chickens to be fed."

"We no longer have any cows here at Meadowsweet," Hallie said crossly, drawing the blankets up around her to shield her body, clad only in her nightgown, from his dark eyes. "Aunt Gwen, you didn't need to prepare a breakfast tray for me!"

"I told her that…that given the late hour, a lunch tray would prove much more appropriate," Trace announced. "Still, after last night, she insisted on allowing you to sleep and on fixing the tray, as well—and because I've always been a sucker for a damsel in distress, what else could I do but carry it upstairs for her, it being way too heavy a burden for her, of course.

"And frankly, it's just as well I did, because in the process, I noticed the carpet runner is loose on one of the steps, that some of those brass carpet rods could really use tightening up."

Carefully setting the tray on Hallie's bed, Trace snatched up the linen napkin, whipping it from its folds and tucking it neatly into the bodice of her nightgown. During the process, he grinned as though he were fully aware of her dismay at his action and of her current reluctance to put him firmly in his place, when Aunt Gwen stood there beaming with delight at the two of them, like some mischievous matchmaking mama from a Regency novel.

"Tea?" he queried, raising one eyebrow mockingly as he gazed at Hallie and deliberately moved to block the elderly lady from her view.

In response, realizing her great-aunt could no longer see her, Hallie childishly stuck her tongue out at him.

"There. I knew that would make you feel better," Trace observed, feigning a deadpan expression as from the china pot on the tray, he poured her a cup of hot Earl Grey tea.

"Yes, indeed. Tea is always the best cure for anything, I always say," Aunt Gwen declared innocently, wholly ignorant of Hallie's behavior and Trace's true meaning.

At that, Hallie nearly choked on the tea she had

drunk from cup he had handed her, and she saw Trace himself was having difficulty keeping his shoulders from shaking with laughter.

"Beast!" she hissed at him, under her breath. "For shame!"

"I have none," he whispered, bending over her, pretending to arrange the tray more closely about her. Then he rose and, in his usual voice, said, "Well, now that's taken care of, I'd best fetch my toolbox and start on those stairs in the main hall."

Had Aunt Gwen not been present, Hallie would have been sorely tempted to fling the teapot at his retreating back. Truly, she did not know what was the matter with her. Richard, her ex-husband, had never aroused such tumultuous emotions in her, making her fingers itch to do him some violent act. But Trace was simply maddening.

It was hard for her to believe she had known him for only a couple of days. Somehow, she felt as though she had known him all her life, had connected with him on some deep level she and Richard had never managed to achieve, despite the two years she had dated him and the three she had spent as his wife.

In the days and then the weeks that soon passed, it was a feeling Hallie was to experience time and again, as she and Trace gradually settled into life and a routine at Meadowsweet. More than once, she was to think they might have been an old married couple, so well were they to work together and so attuned were they to each other's thoughts and wishes.

Still, there were times when he unnerved her, as well, when she remembered that night when he had seemed to her to metamorphose into a wolf, and she entertained weird and perplexing notions about him, wondered if perhaps he were not truly human. Whenever that happened, she could only scowl to herself, thinking that she was undoubtedly letting her imagination run away with her again.

It was sometime after that evening when Hallie had spied Scarecrow peering through her bedroom window that Sheriff O'Mackey returned with the badly disfigured man in tow. She, Trace and Aunt Gwen were out on the verandah, taking a break from their labors and enjoying tall, cool glasses of lemonade when the sheriff drove up.

"Howdy, folks," he greeted them, opening one of the rear doors of his patrol car and ordering Scarecrow to step out. "As you can see, I've caught your intruder, Ms. Muldoon, and now I need to know what you want me to do with him."

As she rose from her chair, Hallie saw that in

broad daylight, the man called Scarecrow, although clearly marred by the warehouse fire from which he had barely survived, was not nearly as frightening in appearance as he had seemed when staring in at her through the window, from the darkness beyond.

Now she could see he was no demon at all, but merely a poor, scarred man, who was plainly frightened by what might happen to him since he had been captured.

"Hello, Scarecrow." Hallie held one hand out to him. "I'm Hallie Muldoon. Will you—will you please tell me why you were spying on me?"

For a long moment he gazed at her outstretched hand as though he were wholly unused to people extending him that common courtesy. Then, slowly, he shook it.

"Please forgive me, ma'am. A whole lot of people are scared of me, because of how I look, and I know you can't think too highly of me... peeking through your bedroom window at you. But I—I wasn't really spying on you, Ms. Muldoon. I heard you'd come back to town, and I—I was just curious about you, that's all. I didn't want you to be upset by my appearance. That's why I came in the dark, so you wouldn't see me. But then I wound up terrifying you, anyway. I'm so sorry.

I never meant to do that. I never meant you any harm."

"I understand. Well, I hope that now we've properly met, you won't feel any need to sneak around here, trying to get a glimpse of me. You must feel free to come here to the house to speak to me whenever you wish."

"Does all that mean you don't want to press charges against Scarecrow, Ms. Muldoon?" the sheriff asked.

"That's right, Sheriff. I believe Scarecrow's explanation, and I don't see what's to be gained by prosecuting him and locking him away somewhere. You've told me he's never hurt anyone here in town, and I don't think he intended me any harm, either." Glancing back at Scarecrow, she continued, "In fact, I believe Scarecrow has already suffered enough for his actions. Were you not attacked by some animal on the verandah, sir—a large black wolf, perhaps?"

"Yes, ma'am—although I don't know whether it was a wolf or not. It was so dark, and the beast came at me so fast that I never really got a good look at it. So I don't know what it was. I just skedaddled as quick as I could. But it still got hold of my leg somehow…gave me a right good nip, it did. So now Doc says I've got to have those rabies shots—in case the creature was rabid. They haven't been able to find it, you know."

"No, I didn't know."

"I did." Trace spoke.

"Oh, you did, did you?" Sheriff O'Mackey glanced with sudden interest at him. "How'd you know that?"

"Only stands to reason. We'd had a thunderstorm the night before Scarecrow came prowling around here. So the ground was still damp and muddy from the rain. That means the wolf would have left tracks—and there weren't any. I checked."

"What do you mean...there weren't any?" A frown of confusion knitted Hallie's brow. "It must have left some sign of its having been here. I mean, *something* clearly bit Scarecrow!"

"I'm not saying it didn't," Trace responded carefully. "I'm just saying that whatever it was, it didn't leave any tracks."

"Well, that just ain't normal!" the sheriff insisted. "What're you telling us, Trace? That this big old wolf simply up and vanished somehow?"

"That's right—and I don't believe you'll find hide nor hair of it, either. Nobody's yet seen it besides Hallie, and while I don't doubt for one single minute that she actually *has* seen it, I think it's her special animal totem, sacred to her alone here at Wolf Creek, and that it won't show itself to another living soul in this town besides her— at least for the time being, anyway."

"Well, no offense, but if you ask me, that sounds like nothing more than a bunch of Indian mumbo-jumbo!" the sheriff declared, eyeing him skeptically. "Animals don't have brains enough to think that way. It's just an exceedingly wiley old wolf, that's all...nothing mysterious or mystical about it. But we'll continue to keep an eye out for it, and sooner or later we'll catch it, sure enough."

"If you say so, Sheriff, then I'm certain you will." Trace smiled pleasantly, but although his expression might have fooled Sheriff O'Mackey, it did not fool Hallie in the least, and she knew Trace did not believe the beast would ever be caught.

Nor, in the days that followed, was it.

Gram's big fat tomcat, Mr. Whiskers, finally put in a much-belated appearance. But even Hallie did not spy the immense black wolf, and she began to wonder uneasily if, in reality, she had only imagined it. But, no, something had bitten Scarecrow— then vanished without leaving a single trace. That part of it, at least, was certainly real enough. So it must be just as Sheriff O'Mackey had said, she told herself firmly. The creature was simply clever enough to elude capture.

It was not some wolf possessed with magical powers, who could come and go like the wind, and who chose to show itself only to her, because it was her special animal totem. She was not even an American Indian.

"That doesn't matter," Trace said, when she mentioned that fact to him. "One way or another, we all have our spirit guides. Some people call them guardian angels, of course, or have other such monikers for them. Regardless of what we know them as, they're sent to watch over us, to serve as our protectors and pathfinders—especially in times of crisis, when we're standing at a crossroads in our life."

Deep down inside, Hallie knew her grandmother had believed much the same thing. But perhaps, despite everything, something of Great-Aunts Agatha and Edith had rubbed off on her, after all—because for whatever unknown reason, Hallie, who had used to dance with faeries in the meadow, stubbornly refused to believe the wolf was anything more than what Sheriff O'Mackey had claimed.

Chapter 13

The Courthouse and the Visitor

In the coming days and then the weeks that passed at Meadowsweet, there was so much to do that Hallie had little time to dwell on the great black wolf and what it might or might not portend.

On Sundays, growing up under the aegis of Great-Aunts Agatha and Edith, she had duly attended church. But once she had got out on her own, Hallie had gradually fallen out of the habit, thinking there were a lot of self-righteous hypocrites sitting in the pews on Sundays, hanging on every word of the service—then promptly forgetting it all once the church doors had closed behind them.

Because neither Aunt Gwen nor Trace was a churchgoer, Hallie saw no reason to start up again herself, and instead, they all took to driving to the cemetery on Sundays, where she and Aunt Gwen laid fresh flowers on the graves of Jotham, Gram and Rowan.

Hallie found the cemetery a peaceful place, and she especially loved looking at all the old gravestones, reading their inscriptions and wondering about the people who lay beneath, what kind of lives they had led upon this earth.

On Saturdays, there was the farmers' market set up around the grassy green square at the heart of town, where all the locals, and sometimes a few out-of-towners, erected stalls from which they peddled fruits and vegetables, and arts and crafts. In wandering from booth to booth, Hallie also took delight, remembering how she had used to play in the square on such days, just as children still did, and to beg Gram for a trinket or two from one of the stalls.

The remainder of the week, there was the hard labor at the farm to keep her busy, along with all the attendant decisions to occupy her thoughts. To ensure there would prove no impediments in the event she determined to sell Meadowsweet, Hallie had her grandmother's last will and testament probated at the courthouse, there furthering her acquaintance with Jenna Overton.

Still, no matter how hard she tried to be pleasant to the heavyset woman, Hallie continued to feel Ms. Overton was a very strange person, and she never felt comfortable in her presence. Nor did it help that whenever she stopped by the courthouse to ask a simple question or two, Ms. Overton, who appeared to be in charge of everything, invariably replied, "I'm not a lawyer, Ms. Muldoon. Therefore, I cannot answer your questions. To do so might be construed as giving you legal advice, and since I'm not licensed by the state as an attorney, it would be illegal for me to act in that capacity."

Regardless of what Hallie inquired about, even seemingly innocuous questions about matters of public record, the response was always the same.

"Really, Aunt Gwen! Jenna Overton is undoubtedly one of the rudest, most unhelpful persons I've ever had the misfortune to meet." Hallie confided as, exiting the courthouse one day, she and her great-aunt headed across the square, intent on doing some shopping at the stores that lined one side of the green.

"She knows that every time I have to send Mr. Winthorpe over to the courthouse, it costs me money, and I believe that's why she deliberately refuses to answer even the simplest, most harmless of questions. I'm *not* asking her to provide me with free legal advice!

"It's just that if I don't keep on top of Mr. Winthorpe, he tends to let things slide, and I want to get Gram's will probated and done with—not keep on having it postponed by one silly delay after another.

"Good grief! Does the entire courthouse grind to a halt every time Judge Newcombe takes a vacation?"

"Well, actually, I expect so, dear," Aunt Gwen said contritely, sympathizing. "I mean, he *is* the only judge in town. So I don't suppose much of anything can be done without him."

"Maybe not," Hallie reluctantly conceded. "Still, one wouldn't think so—the way Ms. Overton behaves. I think she's the one *really* running the courthouse. Why, I'll bet that old goat Judge Newcombe doesn't know even half of what she's doing. She's so bossy and overbearing. She acts like the judge is her own personal property, that she daren't let anyone else even speak to the man!"

"No doubt because Jenna's been in love with

him for years, Hennie always said," the elderly lady explained. "Oh, I know the judge is a good fifteen years or more older than she, and that he's probably never seen her as anything more than a thoroughly competent assistant, besides. Still, I don't think any of that's ever crushed Jenna's strong emotion for him. She worships the ground he walks on.

"From the way she behaves toward you, I believe she's afraid of you, Hallie. After all, you're young and attractive, and I suppose she's got some crazy idea that you'll swoop in and steal the judge away from her. She probably sees every pretty young woman in town as a like threat."

"Good Lord. As though I'd ever be interested in Judge Newcombe! Why, with that pointy bald head, those big ears and that ridiculous beard of his, he looks just like some old billy goat! The few times I've seen him seated on the bench, I've half expected him to bray 'Nyah, nyah, nyah,' just like a goat."

"Oh, Hallie, what a...what a dreadful, disrespectful thing to say." Her pale blue eyes filled with merriment, Aunt Gwen covered her mouth with her hand in a vain attempt to conceal her laughter. "I declare, child, I don't know what the world is coming to, when young people don't have any respect for their elders anymore!"

"People have been saying that since the time of the ancient Greeks, Aunt Gwen, and the world's still here. So I guess it'll just keep marching on, no matter what. Let's go into Coco's Ice Cream Parlour and have a chocolate sundae. Just thinking about Ms. Overton's silly attitude toward me because of Judge Newcombe has got me so riled up that wish I'd never quit smoking. It's times like these when I badly long for a cigarette."

"Yes, but dear, you really shouldn't replace smoking with eating. Still, you've got such a nice slender figure that I don't suppose you have to worry about calories much. It's when you get to be my age that you've truly got to watch what you eat, lest you wind up weighing a couple of hundred pounds or more."

"Oh, Aunt Gwen, you're like a little bird. A chocolate sundae certainly isn't going to hurt *you*, and as for me, I'll just do some extra crunches or something."

In the end, the two women decided to split their sundae, each getting enough of a taste to satisfy her. After that, they completed their shopping, then piled into Hallie's Mini for the ride back to Meadowsweet.

"Who's that, Aunt Gwen?" Hallie queried, as upon reaching the farm at last, she guided the car toward the carport. "I don't believe I've seen that vehicle here before."

"Well, I have."

Much to Hallie's surprise, as she glanced at her great-aunt inquiringly, she saw the older woman's mouth was uncharacteristically thin with dislike and disapproval, so she looked startlingly like Great-Aunt Agatha.

"It belongs to Dandy Don Hatfield—and I'm sorry if it sounds wholly unChristian of me, dear, but I just can't stand him! He's the wealthiest man in town—got rich off selling used cars to people initially, then branched out into all kinds of other schemes—and I'm convinced he's largely responsible for Hennie's stroke!"

"Why? How?"

"Oh, he's been coming out here for years to harass her about Meadowsweet, pressuring her to sell the place to him. He wants to turn it into one of those planned urban developments, with a Victorian theme and using the farmhouse as the model show home. Can you imagine! Why, the first time he explained it all to Hennie, I was afraid she was going to start foaming at the mouth, she was so angry!

"She sent him packing with a flea in his ear, I'll tell you—warning him he'd better not ever set foot on her property again. Still, he kept on coming back here, pestering her, until she finally called Sheriff O'Mackey and had him put a stop to it. But did it stop there? No, it did not!

"For then Mr. Hatfield only waited until he spied Hennie in town, chasing her up and down the streets, shoving contracts into her face and begging her to reconsider—that she'd have enough money after the sale to install herself in one of these luxury retirement homes they've got for elderly people nowadays.

"Anyway, I guess that now poor Hennie's dead and buried, Mr. Hatfield's decided he can persuade you to sell out to him, Hallie. But I'll tell you what, child—I'll be *extremely* disappointed in you if you do!"

"You don't need to worry about that, Aunt Gwen."

As the elderly lady had spoken, a martial glint had come into Hallie's eyes, and already irate about the way Ms. Overton had treated her at the courthouse, she certainly was not going to be bullied at her own home by some used-car salesman who had perhaps harassed her grandmother to death.

After unfastening her seat belt, she got out of the car and strode to the front of the house, where Mr. Hatfield was standing, bending Trace's ear.

As she observed the latter's seemingly casual stance, his battered Stetson hat tipped just so, his thumbs hooked in his wide leather belt, a half-smoked cigarette dangling from one corner of his mouth, Hallie had a good idea that it was all Trace could do to prevent himself from giving Dandy Don Hatfield a thorough thrashing.

"Good afternoon, Ms. Muldoon! Such a genuine pleasure to meet you at last!" Mr. Hatfield greeted her enthusiastically, grabbing her hand before she even offered it and pumping it so hard she thought it was a wonder it did not fall off. "I've heard so much about you from your dearly departed grandmother—God rest her sweet, saintly soul—that I feel I know you already.

"I'm Don Hatfield, but everybody hereabouts just calls me Dandy Don—on account of I'm such a nice fellow!" A wide, gap-toothed grin displaying one gold cap and that did not reach the corners of his steely-gray eyes split his weather-beaten face.

"I'm a car salesman by trade—but don't let that put you off. No, sirree, Ms. Muldoon. Because, for one thing, I can already see you've got yourself quite a smart little vehicle there. A brand-new Mini Cooper S, isn't it? That must have set you back a pretty penny! And, for another thing, I've got a whole lot of irons in a whole lot of other fires besides my car dealership, and it's land I've come to Meadowsweet to speak with you about today."

"My grandmother's farm isn't for sale, Mr. Hatfield," Hallie said flatly once she could get a word in edgewise. "Not today nor any other day. So I'm afraid you've wasted your time driving out here, and quite frankly, I hope it doesn't get to be a habit. I understand you practically hounded my grandmother to death!"

"Now, you—you just hold on a goshdarned minute, young lady!" Mr. Hatfield sputtered, reddening with indignation and ire, his affability disappearing so abruptly that Hallie would have laughed if she had not been so mad.

"I don't know who's been feeding you such a load of cow manure, Ms. Muldoon—although I can no doubt guess—but nothing could be further from the truth, I assure you. The offer I made your grandmother for this place was more than fair— quite generous, in fact—and she was just a stubborn, foolish old woman not to accept it.

"But then, Henrietta Taylor always did think

she was better than anybody else around here, what with her high-society background and her highfalutin airs. Well, she wound up working her fingers to the bone on this old farm—and dropping dead while talking like a loony person to her stupid bees, when she could have been comfortably situated in a luxury retirement home!

"I'm warning you—don't you make the same mistake, young lady! You're liable to wind up dead at Meadowsweet yourself, just like your mother and grandmother!"

Hearing that, Trace suddenly threw his cigarette to the ground and unhooked his thumbs from his belt—like some wolfish predator lithely uncoiling itself, preparing to spring on its prey.

"Are you threatening Ms. Muldoon, sir?" he asked.

His voice was deceptively low and silky, but beneath the brim of his hat, his narrowed blue eyes glittered like such shards in the bright yellow sunlight that Hallie knew she had been right in assessing him as a dangerous man to cross.

"No, I'm simply pointing out the facts to her," Mr. Hatfield insisted, undeterred. "This old farm is way past its sell-by date. Ms. Muldoon isn't going to be able to make it pay, any more than her grandmother was these past years. Places like this simply can't compete with big corporations nowadays, and it hadn't been a lucky home at all for any of her family, besides. Her mama broke her neck here, and now her grandmother's been felled by a stroke. Her daddy knew this place was cursed. Why, that's probably why he upped and ran off!"

By this time, Mr. Hatfield was blustering so loudly that he looked as though he might have apoplexy himself, and he was gesticulating so wildly with one fist that Hallie was afraid he actually meant to strike her.

Warily she took a step back, and at that moment a sudden flash of movement occurred from the side of the house.

At first Hallie thought it must be the massive black wolf, that everyone present would see it at last. But then, as the speeding blur, its head lowered, rammed Mr. Hatfield straight in his large, flabby belly, violently knocking him back into the side of his car, she realized it was Scarecrow who had attacked the man.

"That's not true! That's not true!" the disfigured man screamed, pummeling the startled and now abruptly terrified Mr. Hatfield mercilessly. "Ms. Muldoon's daddy was sorry about running off and leaving her and her mama. He told me so himself!

"He said Meadowsweet was the most wonderful place on earth! So you take that back, what you said about Mr. Muldoon and this here farm, you brainless old overstuffed toad! Or I'll make you sorry you didn't!"

In the end, such was Scarecrow's fury and strength that it was all Trace could do to pull him off Mr. Hatfield.

"If I were you, Dandy Don," Trace drawled insolently, "I'd hurry up and hightail it out of here while you've still got the chance. Scarecrow's so wrought up that, frankly, I don't know how much longer I can hold him!"

Jamming the straw hat he had previously been holding politely in one hand back on his head and swearing mightily, Mr. Hatfield jerked open his car door, got inside his vehicle, then slammed the door shut. Stamping down so hard on the accelerator that his spinning tires caused gravel to spew in every direction, he drove off, sounding just like Arnold Schwarzenegger as *The Terminator* when he hollered out his open car window, "I'll be back!"

Chapter 14

Some Revelations

"Scarecrow, are you all right?" Hallie asked slowly as she glanced at the poor man still pinioned in Trace's tight, powerful grip. "Have you calmed down now? I can't insist that Trace release you unless I'm sure you're not going to do yourself nor anybody else an injury. I thought you weren't a violent man, Scarecrow."

"I'm not, ma'am...I—I promise you," he gasped out, trying to catch his breath. "I—I don't know what...came over me. Ever since I was bitten by that maybe rabid animal, I've—I've just felt so strange, and I was so very angry about that man threatening you, shaking his fist at you, and what he said about this place and your daddy."

"Yes, I'd like to hear more about that, please. Let him go now, Trace. Scarecrow, would you like to join us on the verandah for a cold glass of Aunt Gwen's fresh lemonade? It's become a habit with us to enjoy a pitcher of it every day around this hour."

"I'd—I'd be mighty pleased to, Ms. Muldoon. Thank you ever so kindly."

"Aunt Gwen, would you mind very much getting the lemonade for us? And, Trace, there're some packages in the car, which I'd appreciate you carrying upstairs for me. Now, Scarecrow." Hallie settled herself on the glider and patted the place beside her. "Will you sit here, and tell me about my father? How did you come to know him?"

"It happened—it happened the last time I was in the hospital, Ms. Muldoon," Scarecrow explained. "He was there, too, in the bed next to mine. We started talking, and he told me his name—Liam Muldoon."

"Yes, that was...that was my father's name," Hallie confirmed slowly.

"He told me about this place, Meadowsweet. 'Heaven on earth,' he called it, and he said he had been a real fool ever to leave it, that he'd abandoned his wife and baby, and that now he'd had a while to think about it, it was the biggest mistake he'd ever made in his life. He hadn't been ready for all the responsibilities that come with marriage and a child, he said, but that instead of running away, he ought to have stayed and stuck it out, doing the best he could for his family.

"He told me that if he got out of the hospital—he was very sick, ma'am...with what, I don't know—he was going to come back here. He gave me this." Scarecrow pulled a gold pocket watch from his baggy trousers, handing it to Hallie. "He said he wanted me to keep this, to return it to his wife someday. He made me promise.

"I tried to protest...that I was weak and that since the warehouse fire and all the treatment I'd needed, I was easily susceptible to infection, that I might not survive myself...that he should keep the watch instead and give it to his wife himself. But he insisted." Scarecrow paused for a moment, remembering. Then he went on.

"I wish I could tell you what happened to him, Ms. Muldoon. But the truth is that I simply don't know. I was discharged from the hospital a few days later, and by the time I was well and truly back on my feet and could return there to ask about him, he was no longer a patient. The hospital could find no record of him, either.

"Anyway, I was at loose ends, with nowhere else, really, to go. So I came here to Wolf Creek, to Meadowsweet. But it was a bad time then, filled with pain and grief, for your mother had just died, and your grandmother had sent you away. There was nothing I could do. Still, I stayed on...got me a little place up the road a piece so I would always be near to the farm.

"Then, one day, you came back, Ms. Muldoon. That's why it was so important to me to see you." Scarecrow shrugged simply.

"But you said nothing of all this to me before— when I might have pressed charges against you. Why didn't you speak then?" Hallie asked.

"The sheriff was there. It didn't seem right to talk about this before strangers."

"Thank you...thank you for telling me all this, Scarecrow." Hallie patted his hand, grateful for the story he had told her and feeling the pocket watch, smooth and warm in her palm.

"It's...it's George, Ms. Muldoon...George Chester," he announced shyly. "But it's been so long that anyone's called me that that I'd almost forgotten it myself. Scarecrow's always been my nickname, ever since I was child—on account of my being so scrawny.

"My dad used to say that if I didn't eat more, a strong wind would blow me away, just like it would a scarecrow. The name just stuck. So I've always been happy to answer to it…reminds me of my own dad—may the good Lord rest his soul."

"Well, if you two have finished your chat now, Hallie, how about that lemonade?" Aunt Gwen inquired brightly as she joined them on the verandah, Trace following behind, carrying the tray on which the pitchers and glasses sat.

"Yes, thank you, Aunt Gwen," Hallie replied, smiling. "We're ready for it now, aren't we, Scarecrow?"

"Yes, ma'am. I don't think this day can get much hotter. It's awful nice here on the verandah, with the ceiling fans turning and all the shade."

"Trust me, Scarecrow. It's even better if you're armed with a flyswatter!" Aunt Gwen declared, her laughter tinkling and her dimple peeping. "I confess that if I'd had one handy earlier, I fear I'd have been sorely tempted to use it on Dandy Don! Thank goodness you sent him packing, Scarecrow!"

"I know one thing. No matter what Don said, he'd better not come back here!" Trace growled. "I've never liked the cut of his jib—and now I really don't!"

As the two men and the elderly lady continued to discuss Mr. Hatfield's unpleasant behavior, Hallie rose, walking to one end of the verandah, where she could examine the pocket watch Scarecrow had given her.

Pressing its catch, she opened it, and its chimes began to play a melody she recognized as Beethoven's *Moonlight Sonata*. Inside was a picture of her parents and herself as baby. It was a smaller version of the photograph she had discovered tucked away in the trunk at the foot of her mother's bed, when she and Aunt Gwen had tackled that room.

In the past, Hallie had rarely ever given her father a second thought. She had never known him. It had not seemed he had wanted to know her, either, and she had been content to leave things at that.

But now it appeared her father had perhaps suffered a change of heart, and for the first time, she felt curious about him. She wondered whether he were still alive, if, based on the information she now had, she might be able to locate him.

At the very least, she could enter his name into

a search engine and see if there was anything to be found on the Internet, she thought.

In the meantime, there was his pocket watch to treasure, a tangible connection to him and to her past.

Chapter 15

The Watcher

It was after the day Scarecrow attacked Dandy Don Hatfield in the farm's front yard that Hallie began to suffer the disturbing impression that someone was secretly watching her.

Initially, she thought it must be the immense black wolf.

Once or twice, she even believed she had observed it—only to realize it was other, smaller wolves instead. Those animals ran in packs and seldom approached the farm. So Hallie saw them only in the distance and usually after sundown, when they were occasionally to be spied flitting among the isolated green copses dotting the blooming meadows, or else hiding amid the tall grasses that covered the surrounded countryside.

Now and then the beasts came to the creek to drink—never, of course, to that portion of the serpentine waterway that snaked through town, but rather to the desolate stretches that wound through the open farmland beyond.

But although Hallie watched the packs covertly for some sign of the great black wolf, it was never to be seen, and she thought perhaps it had finally moved on, or perhaps had even died of rabies, if it had fallen prey to that disease.

No, whoever or *what*ever was lurking around the farmhouse, spying on her, it was not the wolf Trace had claimed was her special totem animal.

Under other circumstances, Hallie might have suspected Scarecrow. But ever since the day he had provided her with the information about her runaway father, the disfigured man had come and gone freely at Meadowsweet, having no reason to spy on her, surely.

"Hallie." Leaning the pitchfork with which he had been turning the compost heap, Trace pushed back his hat and sighed. "Sometimes, it's difficult for me to believe you ever lived in a big city. Because I would have thought that experience would have made you a great deal less trusting of people than you actually are.

"Why, just look how you hired me on here that first day! You didn't know anything at all about me, except what I told you. I might have been an ax murderer, for all you knew. I'll bet you never even followed up with Frank Kincaid to ensure I was really who I said I was."

"What's your point?" Hallie asked crossly, knowing this to be the truth. "Aunt Gwen knew who you were and that you'd been working over at Frank's place, Applewood, besides."

"Yes, that's true." Trace nodded. "Still, for all she knew, I might have axed Frank to death right before I drove over to your own farm."

"Good grief, Trace! I come out here to tell you I think I'm being spied on—and all you can do is talk about being an ax murderer! A whole lot of comfort you are. It's not *you* who's lurking around Meadowsweet, furtively watching me, is it?"

"No. I like to do all my looking at you openly—because I like to know you're looking right back." He grinned at her for a moment, then, at her frown, hastily sobered. "I'm sorry, Hallie. I'm only teasing you to try to take your mind off your worries. But I don't guess I'm doing a very good job of it.

"My point was this—all you actually know about Scarecrow is what he told you. For all you *really* know, he mugged your absent father on some city street, knocked him in the head and killed him, and stole his pocket watch and wallet—which is how he got the farm's address."

"That's…that's a terrible thought, Trace." Hallie swallowed hard. "And I—I just don't believe one word of it. Scarecrow's lived in that shack of his for more than two decades now, and evidently he's never done anything ill to anybody in Wolf Creek. Besides, I've made clear to him he's welcome here anytime he pleases. So why would he secretly spy on me?"

"I don't know. But he *did* peep through your bedroom window at three o'clock in the morning that one night."

"He explained all that—and I don't think he lied. No, no, it's somebody else. I'm sure of it. But why would somebody want to sneak around here, watching me? It just doesn't make any sense."

"Unless they wanted to drive you off the place," Trace suggested. "And from what you told me, Hallie, you started having all these feelings about being spied on right after Dandy Don Hatfield came out here to make you an offer on the farm. Frankly, I'm surprised you didn't consider him to begin with."

"Well, actually I did," she admitted. "But honestly, I somehow just couldn't see him tramping around here, hiding in the bushes—particularly in one of those god-awful loud suits of his. I would have spotted him a mile away!"

"Yes, I think you're right about that," Trace agreed. "Still, that doesn't mean the man hasn't changed his clothes for something far more suitable to accomplish his more nefarious activities than peddling used cars. Or, more likely, that he hasn't hired some unknown person to do his dirty work for him. As you mentioned, what reason would anybody else in town have to spy on you?

"You've no other enemies here in Wolf Creek, have you, Sleeping Beauty? There's no one else who would want to lurk around Meadowsweet, making you uneasy enough to forego your beauty sleep and to pack up and sell the farm, is there?"

"No, of course not. And I wish you wouldn't call me Sleeping Beauty! I rise just as early and work just as hard on this farm as you do!"

"I love it when you're angry. Your eyes look just like emeralds—spitting fire."

"Will you please be serious?"

"I am. Oh, about the intruder, you mean? Hallie, I don't want you to worry. I feel quite certain your special animal totem is patrolling the premises, keeping watch over you—as I myself do." Although he continued to smile at her, Trace's eyes were once more sober and earnest.

"What would make you think that great black wolf is still hanging around? Have you seen it?"

"Did I not once say I believed it would show itself to no one but you?"

"Then why do you think it's still here? Have you seen its tracks?"

"It doesn't leave any. Don't you remember?"

"Yes, yes, I know. It's a mythical, magical beast with all kinds of strange powers that enable it to come and go like the wind—or so you would have me believe.

"I'm sorry, Trace. But as I've told you before, I'm not a Native American—not even half Native American—and so, as much as your own personal spiritual beliefs may mean to you, I'm afraid they're part of a religion about which I know little more than you've explained to me, and so I find it difficult to have your faith.

"I simply can't rely for protection on some animal that may—or may not—actually exist, that may, in fact, be nothing more than the product of my own wild imagination."

"It bit Scarecrow," Trace reminded her.

"We don't know that. To use your own line of reasoning, we know only what Scarecrow *said* happened on the verandah that night. For all we really know, he might just as easily have been bitten by a dog or even a raccoon or some other such animal."

"Hoist by my own petard! Nevertheless, having myself actually viewed Scarecrow's injured calf to assure myself the wound was not serious, I think I can safely say he wasn't attacked by a chipmunk! No, whatever nipped him—and it *was* only that, thank goodness, a short light chomp intended as a warning—was quite real.

"Even Scarecrow himself wouldn't have agreed to receive the rabies vaccination if he hadn't been worried about contracting the disease. Fortunately, it's no longer administered via those painful shots in the stomach, but these days is given as a series of five or so relatively painless shots in the arm and the butt.

"Hallie, I confess I don't know what more to say to try to comfort you. I've tried both humor and logic, neither with much success, I'll admit, and I've attempted to reassure you that I take your suspicions seriously and am on my guard. What more would you have me do?" Trace queried, clearly at a loss.

"If I thought it would help," he continued, "I'd take you in my arms and kiss away all your troubles. But no doubt I would only have my ears boxed for my pains!"

"You certainly would!" Hallie retorted tartly with feigned primness, for inwardly she felt her heart race at the prospect, and longed to confess that right now she would adore nothing more than to feel his strong, muscular arms wrapped protectively around her, loving her and keeping her safe always.

"However," she went on, "there is one thing you can do—teach me how to use one of those shotguns in the gun case in the library. I'd feel better if I knew I had some way to defend myself, in the event that anything should occur at the farm. What if you weren't here when it happened? I'd have no means of protecting myself and Aunt Gwen!"

"I'm truly flattered by how you've come to rely on me, Hallie. I mean that sincerely, and I promise you, you won't regret it, that I'll never let you down. And of course I'll teach you how to shoot, if you like. But you must make me a promise if I do."

"What...what kind of a promise?" she asked tentatively, half expecting him impudently to demand a kiss or some other such forfeit.

"Simply this—you must promise me you would never shoot the great black wolf. It would be a terrible sacrilege to kill such a magnificent animal as you have described."

"That's an easy promise to keep, Trace—for I would never harm any animal. Gram believed we were put on this planet as caretakers of all God's creatures, and that's a belief I firmly share."

"As do I, so I'm very glad to hear you say that. Now, why don't you give me a hand with this compost heap? Then, later on this afternoon, I'll teach you how to handle a shotgun."

"You've got a deal. Where's the other pitchfork? Oh, never mind. I see it."

Grabbing the tool, Hallie dug into the hot mound, lifting and turning the debris to help hasten its decomposition.

"Come next spring, we're going to have such wonderful compost for the herb and vegetable gardens!" she declared, without thinking.

"Are you planning on staying at Meadowsweet permanently, then?" Trace's voice was carefully noncommittal.

"I...I don't know yet. Still, I suppose that on

some level, I must be considering it, or else I would never have made that comment. I hope...I hope you're not angry with me, Trace. I know you hoped I might sell Meadowsweet to you—"

"Only because that old Victorian farmhouse and its land speak to me, and I didn't want them to go to someone like Dandy Don Hatfield. But you, now...I can see you growing old here at Meadowsweet, Hallie. Although you might have spent most of your life in a big city, I can tell, now, that you never lost your bond with the land. This place suits you, just as it did your grandmother. I know she'd be so happy to have you home here at long last."

"And what about you, then, Trace? Will you...will you stay on here, as well?" Hallie queried hesitantly. "I confess that despite how insolent and maddening I frequently find you, I've got kind of used to having you around."

"Why, Hallie—" Trace grinned hugely, his midnight-blue eyes dancing as he gazed down at her intently "—that's the nicest thing you've ever said to me. I begin to believe there might actually be some hope for me where you're concerned, after all!"

Chapter 16

Traps

In the days that followed, Trace taught Hallie how to load and fire the shotguns in the gun case in the library, as well as how to clean them afterward and carefully lock them away.

"Always remember," he told her, "it's not the gun that's dangerous. The gun itself is just a tool, like any other. It's the person behind the gun who makes the difference one way or the other, and even an experienced shooter can make a mistake and accidentally shoot something or some*one* he or she didn't mean to. So never point a gun at anything you don't intend to shoot."

"I understand," Hallie said, biting her lower lip gently as she concentrated on the task at hand.

It seemed there was a whole lot more to this shooting business than she had ever before realized. She had thought one simply loaded the gun, aimed and fired. But for one thing, she had never counted on the horrific kickback against her shoulder, which invariably spoiled her aim and left her shoulder bruised and aching.

"You'll get used to it, in time," Trace said, "and once you learn how to compensate for the kickback, your shoulder won't hurt so bad, either. You're doing fine. It just takes practice."

"I think I'm going to need quite a bit of that!"

"Yes, I think so, too." He spoke in her ear, his breath warm against her cheek as he wrapped his arms around her again, helping her steady the shotgun and, with his feet, gently moving her own into a slightly wider stance. "You don't want to be knocked off balance."

But Hallie thought she already had been—and not by anything having to do with the gun, either. It was Trace himself who unbalanced her. His very nearness, the feel of his strong, corded arms around her, was intoxicating, making her feel dizzy and breathless, as though she had run a very long way and could not now get any air into her lungs.

When she inhaled deeply, the scent of him permeated her nostrils, somehow reminding her vividly of the man-beast in her dream, the dark, erotic nightmare that had haunted her slumber when she had first come back to the farm. He smelled of the land, of long-shadowed forests and grassy green meadows, and she thought that if she tasted him, his skin would leave a trace of salt upon her tongue, as well.

She had never before spent so much time in such close proximity to him, and no matter how much she had tried to fight it over the passing weeks, Hallie knew she was highly attracted to him, felt as though if he were no longer to be at Meadow-sweet, there would be an emptiness somewhere deep inside her that would be very difficult to fill.

She was always sorry when the day's shooting lesson ended, and for all his impudence, she thought Trace was, too. Still, it was not as though they were deprived of each other's company, because there were many chores they performed together, lazy afternoons when there was lem-onade to be sipped on the verandah and long evenings when they played cards with Aunt Gwen.

Once in a while, Scarecrow or Sheriff

O'Mackey or some other visitor stopped by, and there was a fourth for bridge. Or Hallie and Aunt Gwen played the piano, and Trace joined in on the guitar or the harmonica; he was equally adept at both. Sometimes they went into Wolf Creek, to take in a movie at the only cinema in town.

In many ways, it was a hard life, from sunup till sundown, an unhurried life filled with simple pleasures—no operas nor symphonies, no ballets nor nightclubs.

Still, Hallie had never felt more alive.

After several weeks at the farm, she no longer even needed an alarm clock. The crowing of old Bernard woke her in the mornings, and it was with a deep sense of inner peace and pleasure that she dressed to feed the chickens and gather the eggs from the nests in the coop.

In fact, she thought as she lay in the middle of the wild meadow where, as a child, she had so often danced with the faeries, life would have been just about perfect—if only Dandy Don Hatfield were not trying to drive her off the farm.

Oh, it simply must be him—or else, much more likely, as Trace had said, someone the man had hired to harass her. For now Hallie was certain she was not only being spied on, but also actively stalked.

It had all started with the poor dead mouse she had discovered one morning, laid upon the back porch.

Aunt Gwen had said the tomcat, Mr. Whiskers, had left it there as a present, to show he was doing his job, guarding the farmhouse and protecting it from small furry invaders. Hallie might have believed it, had not other things even more disturbing began to occur.

At first they had been only little things... misplaced tools, when she and Trace both were always so careful with them, new plants dug up and destroyed, the rain barrels used for irrigating the herb and vegetable gardens overturned and emptied of their water.

But yesterday morning...yesterday morning had been the worst.

Now Hallie shivered just thinking about it.

To drive away the birds that otherwise would wreak havoc on the gardens she was trying so hard to bring back to their former glory, she had asked Trace to make her a scarecrow. Even Scarecrow himself, when he had learned of the plan, had got involved in the creation, insisting on providing the clothes. Hallie and Aunt Gwen had helped with the stuffing of them.

"Make sure you get enough, now," Scarecrow

had told them, laughing, as they had crammed in the hay. "So he isn't so scrawny that he'll blow away in a strong wind!"

Once the scarecrow had been finished, Trace had carefully mounted it on a strong wooden pole and erected it in the gardens. Hallie and the rest had had such fun making the hay man, and for the first time since she had known him, Scarecrow had seemed genuinely happy.

But yesterday morning, when she had gone outside to feed the chickens and to care for the bees, Hallie had discovered the scarecrow was on fire. Even though she had shouted for Trace, and both he and she had hauled buckets of water from the rain barrels, in an attempt to save the hay man, their efforts had proved futile. In minutes, it had been consumed by the flames—a charred figure on a stick.

"Who could have done something so positively horrible, Trace?" Hallie had asked, tears stinging her eyes. "It's so cruel—especially in light of Scarecrow himself having been burned in that warehouse fire. I just can't suspect poor Scarecrow of all these unnerving deeds after this, and I can't believe Dandy Don Hatfield would have thought of something this vicious, either!

"You must be right, and he must have hired

somebody to drive me away from Meadowsweet. But I'll tell you what, Trace—all he's done is to make me real mad. I'll never leave this old farm now. Don Hatfield will never get this place. Not as long as I live! I swear it."

Now, remembering, Hallie knew she had meant what she said.

Her decision made and she herself feeling better than she had ever since all the incidents at the farm had started, she sat up, knowing she ought to get back to the house. Still, Hallie lingered. This was really the first time since coming back to Meadowsweet that she had been on her own at the meadow, all alone to indulge in her daydreams and fantasies.

Getting to her feet and smiling to herself as memories of her childhood here swept over her, she began to hum to herself, an old melodic folk song in a minor key. Then she started to dance, prancing and leaping and whirling amid the butterflies, dragonflies and bees that flitted from flower to flower in the meadow.

In that moment, for the first time in her life since she had left Meadowsweet, Hallie felt totally free and alive, as though all the strictures placed on her by Great-Aunts Agatha and Edith had suddenly fallen away.

Still, after a minute, she realized how silly she must appear to anyone watching, and she twirled to an abrupt stop, all her earlier fears returning to haunt her.

Bending, Hallie picked up the shotgun she had carried with her to the meadow, glancing around warily. How could she have forgotten for even a few minutes the malicious acts that were being committed at the farm by one or more unknown persons?

She had made a full report to Sheriff O'Mackey, of course—for all the good that had done. Naturally, he had duly investigated. But even Hallie had been compelled to admit that beyond the threats made to her by Dandy Don Hatfield, there was little or nothing for the sheriff to go on.

Further, when he had questioned her about Mr. Hatfield's statements, she had been forced to confess he had not actually said anything concrete about doing her any injury.

Sheriff O'Mackey had told her he would have a chat with Mr. Hatfield, and that he would also drive by Meadowsweet occasionally, keeping an eye out. But so far, he had come up empty-handed.

Hallie understood. She and Trace could not patrol the farm 24/7, either, and even if the immense black wolf *were* her special animal totem and protector, as Trace claimed, even it could not be everywhere on the farm at once.

It seemed whoever was carrying out the malevolent acts knew exactly when and where to strike, in order to avoid being detected. That came from watching the farmhouse, of course. If only she and Trace could catch the saboteur in the act!

But Hallie held out little hope of that.

She was fully aware that these days, there were all kinds of technical gadgets that, although ostensibly marketed to the general public for legitimate purposes, actually aided and abetted criminals. These included everything from powerful listening devices to deceitful software for placing phony identification on caller ID displays.

She felt that whoever was spying on the farm must be utilizing at least some of these gadgets, particularly to overhear conversations between her and Trace, even though since the advent of all the trouble, they had taken pains to attempt to keep their own security measures quiet. Not only did they not want to tip off the unknown person or persons committing the dastardly deeds, but, also, they did not want to alarm Aunt Gwen any more than was necessary.

They had not been able to keep everything from the elderly lady, of course. The terrible burning of the scarecrow had prevented that, so even Scarecrow, from whom they had been unable to conceal the destruction, had become aware of the problems at Meadowsweet.

Still, Hallie did not want either her great-aunt nor Scarecrow to worry any more than was necessary. So she had tried to make light of the difficulties.

"Just some bored kids playing nasty pranks, I expect," she had told Aunt Gwen. "You know how teenagers are nowadays. Especially in a small town like Wolf Creek, where there's little for them to do, I think they have too much time on their hands—and of course, I don't believe all those violent video games have helped matters."

"No, you're probably right, dear." The older woman had sighed heavily. "Well, Hallie, if you're sure that's all it is, I'll try not to fret about it too much."

"I'm sure," Hallie had said, hating to lie to Aunt Gwen, but also mindful of how stressed Gram had apparently become over Dandy Don Hatfield's relentless attempts to pressure her into selling Meadowsweet, so that in the end, she had dropped dead of a stroke.

Hallie did not want anything similar to happen to her great-aunt.

Carrying the shotgun at her side, its barrel pointed toward the ground, as Trace had taught her, she started across the meadow toward the worn, now largely overgrown footpath that wound through a shady copse to the farm. After entering the small woods, however, she had not gone far when she was stopped dead in her tracks.

There, blocking her path, standing in the long shadows cast by the branches of the old trees, was the massive black wolf.

Hallie had not actually seen it up close and personal since the night of the thunderstorm, when she had first come to Meadowsweet. Still, it was just as great, impressive, and fierce as she remembered, and as she stared at it, mesmerized, she felt her mouth go suddenly dry and her heart begin to hammer wildly in her breast.

What should she do?

Hallie did not know. She had promised Trace that if he taught her how to shoot, she would not use the shotgun against the magnificent animal, and even now, despite her fear, she was loath to break that vow. Besides, the beast had made no threatening moves toward her.

In fact, much to her surprise, as she continued to watch it warily, it whined anxiously a little. Then it started to circle a small area ahead of her on the footpath, where the grass and bramble were so thick that they had nearly obliterated the trail.

"What—what is it, boy?" Hallie asked softly. "Are you trying to tell me something, to warn me somehow? Trace claims you're my special animal totem, my protector, you know."

The beast gazed at her steadily, its ears pricked up attentively and its head cocked a trifle as it listened to her. Tentatively, it took a few steps toward her. Then it ran back to the same spot, whining and circling before settling back on its haunches, looking at her again, as though waiting expectantly for her to do something.

At last, slowly, Hallie dared to approach, peering into the undergrowth to try to determine what might be wrong and that could explain the wolf's peculiar behavior. Initially she could see nothing. So, still moving carefully, she leaned the shotgun against the trunk of a nearby tree, where she had spied a slender broken branch lying to one side.

Picking up this latter, hoping the animal would not think she intended to hurt it, Hallie poked and prodded the thick brush, screaming with terror as a giant pair of steel jaws suddenly leaped from the undergrowth to snap shut on the bough. As her shrieks pierced the summer air, the wolf bared its teeth and began to snarl ominously, lunging and snapping ferociously at the brutal trap now rendered harmless by her springing it.

"Oh, God," Hallie whispered to herself, horrified.

The trap had not been there earlier. She felt certain of that. But had it not been for the wolf's warning, she would have come along this footpath and stepped right into the vicious steel jaws. She might have wound up losing a foot—or perhaps even an entire leg!

At the realization, she abruptly doubled over and vomited, sick and faint with fear.

Whoever was doing these things at the farm must be utterly deranged, she thought, shivering, knowing that for all that he seemed daily to be growing less furtive and addled, Scarecrow was truly not fully right in the head. *Was* it he who had embarked on this increasingly horrific campaign to drive her away from Meadowsweet?

But if so...why?

Dandy Don Hatfield at least possessed a plausible motive: he wanted to buy the farm and turn it into a planned urban development, erecting houses all over the land where Hallie had played and dreamed as a child. But Scarecrow had no such obvious goal.

No, no matter what, she simply could not believe the disfigured man was capable of anything like this. Nor could she envision the flabby, clearly out-of-shape Mr. Hatfield creeping through the woods to set a trap in the thicket. It must indeed be as Trace had suggested, and the obnoxious, loudmouth man had hired someone—some ruthless, conscienceless thug—to do his dirty work.

But before Hallie could dwell further on these highly disturbing thoughts, Trace was there, evidently having heard her shrill, frightened cries and come running. In his hands he bore an ax he had been using to chop wood or carry out some other chore.

At first, not realizing it was he, Hallie jumped violently, nearly startled out of her skin, and reached for the shotgun that lay close at hand. Then she recognized it was Trace, and a long sigh of relief issued from her lips.

"Hallie, what is it? What's wrong? I heard you screaming."

Mutely she pointed to the steel trap on the footpath.

"It was—it was meant for me, I—I know," she choked out. "The great wolf—oh, he's gone now! But he was here a minute ago, and he saved me—"

Then, suddenly, somehow, she was wrapped in Trace's strong, protective embrace, and he was kissing her wildly, feverishly, with all the pent-up passion he had held in check for so long.

Chapter 17

The Cellar

Her heart leaping with thrilling desire, Hallie kissed Trace back ardently, clinging to him as though for dear life, hoping he would never let her go.

For weeks, she had attempted to fight her deepening physical attraction and her ever-growing emotional attachment to him. But now she could no longer suppress her overwhelming feelings, swept away by the tide of rapture and longing he roused in her.

Her hands crept up to tangle in his glossy black hair, even as his own fingers entwined with her long blond tresses to draw her even nearer. His tongue traced the outline of her mouth before plunging between her tremulous lips, kissing her deeply, feverishly, as though he had longed for this moment forever and now meant to savor it fully.

Her body quickening with passion and swift arousal, Hallie pressed herself against him, touching and stroking him everywhere she could reach, as he did her, his mouth taking hers again and again, his tongue tasting and twisting urgently around hers.

Boldly, Trace ravaged her lips, an exhilarating experience that left Hallie dizzy and made her knees tremble, so she thought she would have fallen had he not held her so tightly and upright, crushing her to him. Although she was a woman grown and wise in the ways of the world, in his arms she felt as weak as child and so pliant that she felt as though all her bones were dissolving inside her as she eagerly molded her body to his.

Beneath her hands Trace felt incredibly strong and powerful, making Hallie aware of her own delicateness and fragility in comparison as he slowly led her away from the steel trap, to a soft, mossy place along the banks of Wolf Creek, where he pulled her down and stripped away her clothing before casting off his own. Naked, then, they lay together, bodies entwined, flesh against flesh, seeking and finding closeness and desire.

Time turned—and kept on turning. But Hallie was scarcely cognizant of its passing as she reveled in Trace's embrace. Beneath the canopy of the woods that seemed like a forest primeval, the sweet green moss felt cold and damp beneath her skin, but she was hardly conscious of that, locked in the warmth of his corded arms. She relished the feel of him, his darkly tanned body sleek and taut with muscle, and filmed with a fine sheen of sweat that tasted of salt upon her tongue.

He intoxicated her. She was like fire and ice, burning and melting beneath him as his tongue suckled her swollen breasts, pebbling her nipples and sending waves of electric sensation radiating from them in all directions. The secret heart of her ached for fulfillment, and at long last, he entered her, driving hard and deep into her core.

As Trace penetrated her, Hallie gasped, then cried out, clinging to him fiercely as the two of them became one, pressed breast to breast, thigh to thigh, parting and then meeting again and again in an age-old mating ritual known to every man and woman since the beginning of time. His hands were beneath her hips, lifting her to accept each powerful thrust, until she felt the world spin away into the seemingly mysterious, magical mists that had crept from the creek to enwrap the two of them in their own private cocoon.

As Hallie's own climax shook her, Trace reached his own, his hands tightening on her almost painfully, heightening the intensity of their pleasure. He groaned, then inhaled sharply, jerking violently against her before, finally, he lay still, his heart thrumming furiously against her own.

Quietly they lay together in the afterglow until, eventually, they recognized that the hour was growing late. They dressed and stood then, Trace holding Hallie against his broad chest, caressing her hair gently.

"We've got to call the sheriff and file a report about that steel trap, Hallie," he insisted softly. "I love you—and I don't intend to lose you to whatever maniac is committing these crazy acts."

"Oh, Trace, I love you, too!" Smiling tremulously, she looked up at him tenderly, her heart in her eyes. "And I don't want to lose you, either, nor to fall prey myself to whoever is doing these awful things. If it hadn't been for the wolf—"

Abruptly breaking off, she glanced around wildly for a moment, immensely disappointed but somehow unsurprised when she discovered the animal was still nowhere to be found.

"He's not returned. But it was he who warned me about the trap," she explained. "If not for that, I would doubtless have stepped right into it! He *is* real…the wolf, I mean. I know that now—and perhaps he really *is* my special animal totem, as you've claimed. For it was clear he intended me no harm, when he might have attacked me savagely, but rather wanted only to protect me. I don't know how nor why he's come into my life, but I'm very grateful he has."

"So am I. Come on, Hallie. Let me take you back to the house. I want to be sure you get there safely, that there are no more traps set along the route home." Briefly Trace paused. Then he continued.

"What a terrible way to end the afternoon in your meadow." His blue eyes were filled with love and concern as he gazed down at her. "Aunt Gwen told me earlier where you'd gone. She said your grandmother had told her that was always your special place as child."

"Yes…yes, it was," Hallie confirmed, taking secret delight in how he kept one arm wrapped companionably around her waist as they walked toward the old farmhouse together.

Once there, it was Trace himself who phoned

Sheriff O'Mackey to report what had occurred, while Aunt Gwen, instinctively recognizing something was wrong and demanding to be told what had happened, clucked and fussed over Hallie, settling her in the swing on the verandah and pouring her a glass of lemonade.

"I'd just now finished making it." The elderly lady chattered on brightly, as though trying to take Hallie's thoughts off the terrible steel trap.

But nothing could do that, of course.

Even now, in her mind, she could still see its great, powerful jaws springing up at her, and inwardly, she shuddered. Her fear was mitigated only by the knowledge that Trace loved and desired her, that they had consummated their relationship—that were it not for the dreadful trap, he might never have been emboldened to speak or she to answer.

Still, she was old and wise enough to realize people often said things in the heat of a moment that they did not mean, and she hoped she had not made a mistake in giving herself to Trace or baring the secrets of her heart to him.

But much to Hallie's happiness, in the days that passed, he made it plain he did not intend their relationship to be nothing more than a summer fling, that he wanted her forever and always, and intended to marry her if she would have him.

"Oh, Trace, of course I will," she responded when he asked her.

"Are you sure, Hallie? I mean, I know you've already had one unhappy marriage...."

"Yes, I know. But this time, things are different. This time, I'm sure. You're the man for me, Trace Coltrane, now and for all time. I neither want nor need any other."

He kissed her deeply then, and in her heart she could sense Gram's delight and approval, and she felt somehow that even Great-Aunt Agatha was pleased.

"Oh, my God," Hallie breathed after a long while. "I forgot to tell the bees!"

Flinging back his dark head, Trace laughed.

"Come," he said. "We'll tell them together."

Hand in hand, they walked to where the white wooden hives were lined up neatly in a row behind the old farmhouse, and they spoke to the bees about their plan to be married, and also of their hopes and dreams for Meadowsweet.

After that, they returned to work on the flower beds clustered thickly around the base of the house.

All summer long, Hallie had put off tackling these, insisting that because they were purely ornamental, so served no useful purpose beyond delighting the beholder's eye, they should be set on the back burner for the present, not take precedence over things that were clearly of far more importance. But following the incident with the trap, Trace had said that since the flower beds were so wildly overgrown, they now constituted a hazard, because they provided a haven for the setting of further traps—or, worse, for someone to hide in, bent on doing Hallie some harm.

"I'm not going to be fool enough to give somebody prime cover for lurking around the house, Hallie," he had stated firmly. "All that evergreen shrubbery, especially, is just jam up against the windows on the side of the house, and that unbelievable tangle of English ivy has got so thick that we'd be damned lucky to see any trap hidden in there."

"Yes, you're right, of course," she had agreed.

So, earlier that morning, armed with hoes and rakes, they had set about to rectify the situation. Even Aunt Gwen had pitched in with a pair of pruning shears, mercilessly cutting back lilac and rosebushes and deadheading flowers.

Now, as Hallie yanked brutally at the tough, pervasive strands of ivy that gripped the ground and clung to the sides of the house, she thought perhaps she ought to have undertaken this particular task earlier, before it had grown even worse. The ivy's suckers had punched myriad tiny holes into the wood siding that covered the farmhouse and done damage, as well, to its brick foundation.

Tossing the tendrils aside, she bent to make a closer inspection of this last, her heart abruptly beginning to pound hard in her breast at what she saw.

"Trace! Aunt Gwen! Come here! Quick! What does that look like to you?"

"It looks—" Trace spoke, after rising from his own examination "—as though at some point in time, your grandmother had the cellar windows bricked in."

"No! I didn't know this old farmhouse had a cellar!" Aunt Gwen exclaimed, an astonished and perplexed frown knitting her brow. "Hennie never said a single word to me about that. And why would she have had its windows all bricked up to conceal it that way?"

Suddenly Hallie knew—without warning, a fearsome, long-suppressed memory rushing to engulf her, snatching away her breath and leaving her trembling with horror.

"I know. I remember!" she cried, utterly stricken, her lovely countenance ashen.

Turning on her heel, she raced inside the house, down the main hall to the bright, cheerful kitchen that had so strangely haunted and bothered her ever since her arrival at Meadowsweet. Like a madwoman she started grabbing the crockery from the shelves of the huge old Welsh dresser that stood against one wall.

"Help me!" she pleaded with Trace and Aunt Gwen as they appeared in the doorway, their faces evidencing their puzzlement and concern. "Please. Help me!"

Together, then, they rid the shelves of the crockery. Then Hallie started to tug wildly at one side of the massive piece of furniture.

"Let me do it, Hallie," Trace commanded gently. "I know you're a strong woman, but still, it's far too heavy for you."

While he hauled the heavy dresser away from the wall, Hallie ran to fetch a hammer from the toolbox in the pantry. When she returned to the kitchen, Trace had got the big piece of furniture moved out of the way, and with a mighty whack, she smashed the hammer into the plasterboard, sending chunks of gypsum flying.

"Hallie! Hallie, child, what are you doing?" Aunt Gwen asked, eyeing her askance.

"The cellar door used to be right here! That's what was missing from the kitchen. I never could figure it out until now."

"Yes, but dear, surely, there's no need for this—this frenzied destruction. Or even to open the cellar up at all right now. It's not as though we need it. I'm sure it was originally meant only for storing roots or coal—"

"*I* need it, Aunt Gwen! I need to see it! It's where Mom died…on the cellar steps—not on those in the main hall, the way Gram always said," Hallie got out excitedly, between determined bursts of hammering the plasterboard.

"I remember now! I *was* inside that day! Mom and I were playing hide-and-seek, and I'd come inside to the kitchen and climbed into the cabinet under the old copper sink. I was small enough then to fit inside. But it was dark in the cupboard, so I'd left the door open just a crack, so I wouldn't be scared and so I could see if Mom were getting close to finding me, besides.

"But when she finally appeared in the kitchen, she had somebody with her. They were arguing and—and, oh, God, Mom didn't accidentally fall down the cellar steps. She was *pushed!*"

Chapter 18

Rowan's Murder

Hearing Hallie's tearful accusation, Trace, who had momentarily been standing there in just as much confusion as Aunt Gwen, was abruptly galvanized into action. With his bare hands he grabbed exposed edges of the plasterboard and jerked it violently from the wooden studs, throwing the huge pieces into a pile in one corner.

In short order, he and Hallie had got the wall torn down.

The door to the cellar had been removed before

the resulting hole had been plastered over. So there was nothing besides the studs themselves to block Hallie's view of the steep narrow flight of stairs that disappeared into the dank darkness beyond.

Fetching the flashlight from the pantry, Trace switched it on, shining its bright beam down the steps to reveal the cellar's old brick walls, damp and coated with a pale green film.

"It's just as well you exposed all this," he told Hallie grimly. "Because it will need cleaning up and waterproofing. You want to go down there, I take it?"

"Yes, I do." She nodded, swallowing hard. "Please don't try to stop me."

"I promise you, I had no such intention."

Maneuvering his way through the studs, he climbed partway down the steps, then extended his hand to her.

"Oh, Hallie, I know how extremely important this is to you, dear. But please be careful," Aunt Gwen entreated.

"Don't worry. I will be, Aunt Gwen. Besides, Trace won't let me fall."

"No, I won't," he insisted quietly. "Take your time. These stairs are treacherous. It is no wonder they proved fatal to your mother."

Carefully Hallie slipped between the studs to

descend the steps to the cellar below. She and Trace went down slowly, fully aware the long-unused wooden staircase was rickety—and that it possessed no hand rail, besides. Only ever just a thin strip of pine to begin with, the original hand rail had shattered when Rowan had fallen to her death so long ago.

Hallie remembered the terrible cracking sound the wood had made when it had broken, the noise mingling horribly with her mother's long, anguished wail of shock and horror.

And, then, the silence.

That had been the worst thing of all to the child who had crouched, utterly terrified, in the cabinet beneath the old copper sink, her heart beating so fiercely that she had felt it would burst from her breast. She had scarcely even dared to breathe, for fear her mother's killer would hear her and murder her, too.

She had still been hiding there, huddled up in a pathetic small ball, when Gram had returned home and discovered her and her mother's body.

In between the sobs that had racked her entire tiny being, Hallie had stammered out her tale of terror to her grandmother. But in the end, despi‍ all her grandmother's quiet questions, Halli‍

been unable to say with whom it was Rowan had quarreled.

"I don't know, Gram! I don't know! I didn't see! Really, I didn't!"

"All right. All right, child. There, you mustn't think about it anymore. You mustn't think about it ever again!"

Despite her own deep shock and grief over the brutal murder of her daughter, Gram had fought fiercely to protect the granddaughter she had loved and cherished so much.

"You must speak of what happened to no one, Hallie," her grandmother had told her gravely. "For if whoever killed Rowan ever learns you witnessed the murder, your own life will be in mortal danger, as well. Do you understand?"

That was why Gram had sent her away immediately after her mother's death, of course, Hallie understood now. So she would be safe.

So no one would ever question Hallie, Gram had falsely informed the sheriff she had returned home to find Rowan dead at the foot of the stairs. Hallie had been off chasing butterflies in her favorite meadow all afternoon and so knew nothing, Gram had lied, and after a brief inquiry, Rowan's fall had been written off as a terrible, tragic accident.

Afterward, Gram had sealed up the cellar and redone the kitchen, and when people had inquired about her daughter, she had said briefly that Rowan had fallen down the stairs. Gradually over the years, people had forgotten about the cellar and eventually come to think it was the staircase in the main hall that had led to Rowan's untimely death. That was how Hallie had got so confused about it.

Who had murdered her mother? she wondered anxiously now. For the answer to that was the one thing she could still not recall, no matter how hard she tried.

As she stared down at the brick floor where her mother had lain, she could see a dark patch of discoloration, and she knew it was her mother's blood, born of the deep wound Rowan had suffered when her head had struck the stairs.

Hallie shuddered uncontrollably at the thought, and comfortingly, Trace drew her close, kissing the top of her head gently.

He shone the flashlight into the far dark reaches of the cellar, but there was nothing but emptiness and a few forgotten chunks of coal to be seen. If there had once been anything here that would have told her who killed her mother, it was long gone.

"I want to go back upstairs now," Hallie said, clinging to Trace, hot tears stinging her eyes.

"We'll need to call Sheriff O'Mackey. I've got to tell him what I saw that day. Gram wanted justice for Mom. I know that now. That's one of the reasons why she left me the farm. After so many years of deliberately helping me to suppress my memories of that terrible afternoon, she hoped that if I came back, I would finally remember what happened...who it was who murdered my mother."

"Do you know now?" Trace queried, his dark visage sober and filled with love and concern for her.

"No." Hallie shook her head. "I told Gram the truth that day. I never actually saw who it was Mom argued with, who pushed her down the cellar stairs."

"Hallie, I don't know if you've yet realized it, but...all these malicious things that have been occurring here at the farm...maybe they don't have anything at all to do with Dandy Don Hatfield wanting to buy the place. Maybe because you've come back to Wolf Creek, whoever murdered your mother has figured out you were a witness that afternoon, that that's why your grandmother so hurriedly packed you off to your great-aunts back East. Maybe the killer still lives in town and fears to be exposed after all this time, so has been attempting to drive you away."

"Yes," she agreed slowly. "But, then, who could it be? Surely, in that case, it doesn't have anything to do with Mr. Hatfield! Oh, I wish I hadn't been so scared that afternoon, that I'd seen who Mom was quarreling with, that at the very least, I could recall what their argument was about. Because somehow, I think if I remembered that, I would know who murdered her."

"I know it's difficult, but try not to dwell on it, Hallie, and perhaps it will come to you," Aunt Gwen suggested as Hallie and Trace reached the top of the steps. "Oh, dear, I know this hasn't been anything but positively traumatizing for you.

"Sit down, child, and let me fetch you a glass of that apricot brandy. Trace, you'd better get Sheriff O'Mackey on the phone. Whether he likes it or not, he's going to have take all these mean incidents here at the farm seriously now—not just write them off as kids' pranks!"

Eventually, in response to Trace's call and brief explanation, the sheriff arrived to take Hallie's statement, as well as to examine the cellar steps and the old bloodstain at its foot.

"I was only a young deputy in those days, but I remember when Rowan died. We didn't have any reason back then to think it was anything more than the accident your grandmother claimed, Ms.

Muldoon. I know she loved you and was only trying to protect you, but she shouldn't have made you keep quiet about what you saw that day."

Sheriff O'Mackey's face expressed his disapproval.

"The trail's gone cold now. We're more than twenty years down the road now, and in the meantime—although I can understand why she did it—your grandmother's remodeled the entire kitchen, destroying any evidence there might have been, and sealed up the cellar, leaving it to go all dank and moldy, to boot!

"I don't mind telling you folks it'll be difficult, if not damned nigh impossible, now to find any proof beyond Ms. Muldoon's word about just exactly what happened that afternoon!"

"Does that mean you're not even going to investigate this matter, Sheriff?" Trace asked coolly.

"Hell, no. I dated Rowan once or twice when we were teenagers, and I always liked her. So if there's any justice to be had for her, I'm damned well going to find it. I remember a couple of things, too, from back then," the sheriff stated. "Like how mad Don Hatfield was, for instance, that Rowan wouldn't marry him after your daddy ran off, Hallie.

"Maybe *that's* the real reason he's long been after this old farm! Maybe he came here that afternoon, quarreled with your mama, killing her, and has lived in fear ever since that his crime would come to light someday. Maybe he really wants this place so he can cover up any evidence he thinks may still be remaining."

"Oh, God, I didn't know that about Mr. Hatfield and Mom. What a hideous thought."

"Well, it's the truth," the sheriff insisted. "Dandy Don had been after her for years. But don't you worry yourself none about it, because your mama never did give him the time of day. No, there was somebody else she was seeing, I think—although I don't recollect who it was.

"I mean, she'd waited the seven years necessary to have your daddy declared legally dead, and she was still a young, beautiful woman at the time. So she was entitled to a life of her own and some happiness after that."

Closing up his spiral-bound notebook, the sheriff sighed heavily.

"I'm sorry I can't make you folks any promises—except one. I'll do my best," he vowed.

"We can't ask you for any more than that, Ned," Aunt Gwen said, her weather-beaten face troubled and thoughtful as she closed the front door behind him—only to be compelled to answer the back door a few moments later.

Scarecrow stood outside.

"I saw Sheriff O'Mackey was at Meadowsweet again," he greeted the elderly lady. "He passed by my place on his way here, and I got worried. Has something else happened?" His eyes widened as he peered inside and observed the destruction in the kitchen.

"Yes, Scarecrow. Come on inside, and we'll tell you everything." Aunt Gwen stepped aside to let him pass.

Opening one of the kitchen cupboards, she removed the bottle of apricot brandy and four snifters, pouring the alcohol into the glasses and handing them out as Hallie and Trace explained to Scarecrow everything that had come to pass that day.

For a long minute afterward, he just sat at the kitchen table mutely. Then at last he spoke.

"I—I have a confession to make," he announced, his voice hoarse with emotion. "And I hope you all don't hate me for it—because even with all that's happened, these last several weeks, since Hallie came to Meadowsweet, have been some of the happiest of my entire life."

"Oh, Scarecrow, please don't tell me you're about to say you murdered my mother! I—I don't believe I could bear that!"

Hallie gazed at him pleadingly, realizing in that moment how much she had come to like and care for the poor disfigured man.

"No, no." Scarecrow shook his head. "I didn't kill Rowan. But I—I was here that awful day."

"What?" she cried, dismayed.

"You see, I—I lied to you, Hallie. My name's not actually George Chester. I just told you that because I was ashamed to tell you the truth. I know I don't have any rights at all where you're concerned—and really, I wouldn't blame you if you despised me and put me off Meadowsweet at once. But I'm—I'm Liam Muldoon...your daddy, Hallie."

"What?" she exclaimed again, utterly astounded, not certain she could stand any more shocks today.

"It's true. I've got all the necessary papers to prove it—and letters from your mama, too. Some of what I told you *was* the truth. I was hospitalized, obviously, and lying there in that hospital bed, with no one to give a damn whether I lived or died, I *did* come to realize what an inordinately stupid mistake I'd made in abandoning my wife and baby.

"So after I got out of the hospital, I wrote to Rowan, explaining to her how I'd been burned in the warehouse fire and didn't know if I were going to survive, but that before I died—if the good Lord chose to take me—I wanted her to know how much I'd loved her and you, Hallie, and how sorry I was at making such a real mess of things.

"Much to my surprise—because I sure didn't expect any reply—Rowan wrote back to me, and before I knew it, we were corresponding, and I was remembering all the reasons why I had fallen in love with her in the first place. Above all, she was a very kind woman, your mama was, and even though I didn't deserve it, she forgave me for everything and asked me if I wanted to come home."

Scarecrow paused, reflecting. Then he continued.

"By then, she'd already had me declared dead, of course. But that wouldn't have mattered, because I hadn't had any life-insurance policy or anything like that. I warned her I wasn't the same man, that I—I looked like monster now. But Rowan said that was all right, that at the very least, I should be a part of your life, Hallie.

"I—I just can't tell you how horrible it was…finally arriving at Meadowsweet, only to find her lying dead at the foot of the cellar stairs. It was the worst day of my life. I didn't know what to do. I looked for you, Hallie, but you were nowhere to be found, and then I realized you wouldn't know who I was, anyway, even if I hadn't been burned and disfigured.

"I was afraid the authorities would think *I* had killed Rowan. So I did what I'd always done when faced with hard decisions—I ran away again," Scarecrow admitted bitterly, clearly ashamed and riddled with guilt. "Still, I didn't stay gone long. I had made a promise to myself and to Rowan, and for once, I was determined I was going to keep my word.

"So, after she was buried, I came back, pretending I'd only just arrived in Wolf Creek, and here I've been ever since, hoping you'd return one day to Meadowsweet, Hallie.

"Can you—can you ever forgive me, daughter? You don't have to acknowledge me as your father or anything like that. I can understand if that's not what you want. But please don't send me away...just let me come here sometimes to see you still, and let me know if there's any way I can ever help you, if you ever need anything. I've tried to watch over you as best I can since all these bad things started occurring here at the farm...."

"I—I don't know what to say," Hallie said. "Truly, I'm stunned by all these revelations. But of course I won't send you away! You're my father, and I've—I've come to care a lot about you over these passing weeks. If Mom could forgive you, I'm sure I can. I'd love to see her letters to you. Will you show them to me sometime?"

"Yes." Scarecrow nodded humbly. "Yes, I will. Thank you, Hallie. You won't ever again regret having me for a father, I promise you!"

Chapter 19

The Killer

For the first time since that first night she had come to Meadowsweet, Hallie was alone at the old farmhouse. Believing the older woman had needed something to take her mind off her worries, she had urged Aunt Gwen to go to lunch with Blanche Winthorpe, and Trace had driven into Wolf Creek to fetch much-needed supplies.

Because she had been going into town, too, he had wanted Hallie to accompany him. But she had told him she did not know how long she was going to be tied up with Simon Winthorpe that morning at the courthouse, where, after one delay after another, the probating of Gram's last will and testament was finally coming to an end.

So Hallie had driven her own car into Wolf Creek and had only just now arrived back home, glad she was not ever again going to have to bother speaking anything more than a polite greeting to Jenna Overton. The odd, heavyset woman was positively cuckoo! Hallie thought.

Every time Judge Newcombe had addressed Hallie in court today, Jenna had stared daggers at her—despite the fact that by this time, everybody in town knew Hallie was engaged to marry Trace and that, just last weekend, he had presented her with a simple but beautiful diamond engagement ring, which she now wore always on her left hand.

"As though I'd ever be interested in that bald, pointy-headed old Judge Newcombe!" Hallie muttered crossly to herself now. "As though *any* woman besides Jenna herself would be! Doesn't she realize she's more than welcome to him, that nobody else in town has any designs whatsoever on that old goat?"

Taking off the sun hat she invariably wore to please Aunt Gwen, Hallie called out, "Dad? Dad, are you here?"

Ever since learning Scarecrow was really her long-lost father, Hallie no longer addressed him by his childhood nickname. She knew how much it pleased him to hear her call him Dad, and after much reflection, she had decided that whatever wrongs he had done her and her mother in the past, he had more than paid for them, and tried to set matters right. So Hallie did not have it in her heart to hate him.

"Dad?" she called again, wandering through the house, wondering where he was.

He was supposed to come over sometime today, to help her harvest the honey from the beehives, and she had told him that if he arrived at noon, she would fix him lunch.

Glancing at the clock in the kitchen, to which she had returned, Hallie saw it was just now that hour. Maybe her father would arrive in a few minutes. She would get started on lunch and hope he presently showed up. One thing she was certain of—unless he had suffered some unforeseen calamity, he would not stand her up.

Grabbing ham, Swiss cheese, lettuce and mayonnaise from the fridge, Hallie put them on the long farmhouse table at the heart of the room. Then she selected a couple of fresh tomatoes from the vegetable garden from the bowl on the counter, humming cheerfully to herself as she worked. A loaf of freshly baked bread from the bread box was the last thing she needed before preparing the sandwiches.

But when she finally turned back to the table, the bread loaf in hand, Hallie abruptly froze, horrified at the sight that met her suddenly wide, frightened green eyes.

Jenna Overton stood in the kitchen, a peculiar, blank expression on her pudgy, unattractive face.

"What—what are *you* doing here, Jenna?" Hallie queried slowly, the wheels of her brain churning furiously. "How—how did you get in?"

"I had a key to the back door, of course." Jenna held up the key ring she had used to gain entry. "I took it off that old scarecrow who now claims to be your father."

"Dad! Is he all right? What did you do to him?"

"Gave him a crack over the skull, with an old pipe I found in the barn. He's probably dead now. But you, Rowan...you just won't die, will you?" the woman went on tonelessly, not even seeming to realize she had confused Hallie with her mother.

Jenna Overton must undoubtedly be insane, Hallie thought, now realizing that the woman was not merely unpleasant, but actually dangerous. She had surely murdered Hallie's mother.

"I thought I had got rid of you more than twenty years ago, Rowan," Jenna continued, confirming Hallie's worst fears. "I warned you to keep away from Billy, didn't I?"

Ironically, given how much he resembled a goat, "Billy" was Judge Newcombe's Christian name.

"But you just wouldn't listen, would you? Oh, you claimed it was somebody else you were secretly involved with and that you hoped to be reunited with him soon. But I knew you were nothing but a liar and a tramp, that it was Billy you had your heart set on, when you knew he was mine.

"Now you've come back to Wolf Creek, to try to steal him away from me again! No, don't bother to deny it! I saw how you looked at him in court this morning! You couldn't take your eyes off him, could you? Practically drooling over him, you were! Well, I won't have it, I tell you. So I've got to take care of you once more, just as I did before."

Terrified as the short, overweight, but plainly strong woman started to move toward her, Hallie glanced around wildly for a weapon. She did not think she could safely get around the long farmhouse table to either the library and the gun case, or to the back door.

She was worried sick about her father's well-being, and, at the moment, equally concerned about her own welfare. Her only ray of hope was that Jenna did not appear to possess a weapon either, and at that realization, Hallie was quick to grab a sharp butcher knife from the wooden block on the farmhouse table, brandishing it threateningly.

"You'd better keep away from me!" she warned. "I'm not Rowan! I'm her daughter, Hallie, and I didn't grow up here, but in a big city back East, where we know how to defend ourselves! I'll use this if I have to. So please don't make me hurt you. Just get on out of here, and I'll forget you ever came here!"

"More lies, as usual. Do you think I'm an idiot? Everyone else in town might fall for your act, Rowan, but I'm wise to your tricks. I've seen how you deceive men—leading them on with your pretty blond hair and your emerald-green eyes, twisting them around your little finger and making complete fools out of them! You had so very many. Why couldn't you leave Billy alone?"

Before Hallie realized what the madwoman intended, Jenna suddenly lunged across the farmhouse table, grabbing hold of Hallie's wrist and beating it furiously against the edge of the table, forcing her finally to let go of the knife. Then, despite how hard Hallie fought against her, the woman slowly hauled her across the table, jerking her to her feet, then dragging her toward the gaping hole in the kitchen wall, where the cellar stairs waited menacingly.

Desperately, Hallie bit and clawed and kicked her assailant, wondering if Jenna's beefy hands would strangle her—or break her neck—before throwing her violently down the dark dank steps, just as they had so brutally flung her mother down.

The woman was squeezing Hallie so tightly that she felt as though her rib cage were being crushed, and that all the air was being forced from her lungs. She could not breathe!

Then, just when she thought she was going to pass out from lack of oxygen, Hallie heard a ferocious snarl, and without warning, the great black wolf tore through the screen door, bolting into the kitchen and grabbing hold of Jenna as though she were a plump rag doll from which he meant to devour every last ounce of stuffing.

As Hallie stumbled free, screams erupted from her throat to mingle with those of the other woman, who had been ruthlessly pulled to the floor by the maddened animal and was now being mercilessly savaged by it.

"Oh, God, oh, God," Hallie moaned, petrified,

realizing the immensely powerful beast meant to kill Jenna, perhaps would rip out her jugular vein at any moment.

Then, just when she thought the woman's crazed, obsessed life had come to a violent end, Hallie heard a high, sharp whistle, and to her everlasting surprise, the massive wolf suddenly fell back as though he had been shot, his muscular haunches still quivering with adrenalin, his keenly attuned ears alert, his throat still growing fiercely.

Much to her relief, Trace stood in the doorway, armed with a stout pipe, along with her father, who sagged weakly against the ripped screen door, blood trickling down his scarred face from the wound on his scalp.

Somehow, Jenna was still alive, lying bloody and groaning on the kitchen floor. When she attempted to rise, Trace snarled at her to be still, sounding as fierce as the wolf and informing her that if she moved, she would get a worse crack upside the skull than she had given Hallie's poor father.

"Stand guard, Beowulf," he ordered the wolf, much to Hallie's surprise and sudden confusion and wonder. Then, turning to her, he directed, "Get the phone and call Sheriff O'Mackey, sweetheart. Tell him the justice due for your mother's murder is at long last now at hand."

Epilogue

In the Still of the Night

Once, the great black wolf had been a poor, scrawny animal, injured and half starved, desperate to survive a hard, bitter winter. Stumbling through the snow, he had happened upon an old farmhouse.

There, an old woman had spied him, and rather than run away in fear, she had treated him kindly, tending his wounds and feeding him slabs of raw meat.

Like all those of his ilk, he had understood she

was a creature of the earth, one of the few of humankind who had not lost touch with the old ways, when man and beast had respected one another and lived in harmony with the land.

So, gratefully, he had accepted the woman's ministrations, and when he had grown stronger, leaving her to make his own way again in the world, he had not forgotten her, but determined to watch over her and protect her always.

She had called him Beowulf, "because," she had told him, "that's who you remind me of," and she had recounted to him the tale of the great warrior, while the wolf had listened attentively to the sound of her mellifluous voice washing over him. It had been a rich earthy voice that had pleased him to hear, just as he had delighted in the woman's equally unbridled laughter.

Like her old tomcat, he had come and gone at the farm, and she had never tried to restrain him. But then, one day, after casting a magic circle and bewitching him, the old woman had been gone, and the wolf had known she had passed beyond the veil of gloaming only he and those who were one with the land could still see.

But she had left behind a granddaughter, and so it had become the wolf's mission to guard the young woman, just as he had stood sentry over her grandmother.

Now, as he cocked his intelligent black head a trifle, his ears pricking at the sound of the young woman's voice on the verandah, where she sat with her husband, Trace, and with her father and Aunt Gwen, the wolf could sense her deep happiness.

Life was good, Beowulf thought, and in his mind—for their thoughts were one and had been ever since the night Gram had cast her spell of enchantment upon them—he heard Trace silently agree.

Theirs was a special bond that they would share until death now, just as they would always protect Meadowsweet farm and all who lived there—especially Hallie, who held their hearts safe in her keeping and would forever more. Just as they were bound to each other, so they were bound to her. In the beginning, it had been Gram's powerful spell that had enchanted them and drawn them to Hallie. But now, it was far more than that—a deep and abiding love for her that transcended the ordinary. She had trusted them both, given them her own heart, wholly and freely, and more—for she, too, had believed in the magic to be found at the old farm, and she had cast her own circle and made them a part of it for all time.

After listening intently for a moment longer to Trace's thoughts about the power of love and magic, the wolf nodded in accord, then lowered his head to his huge paws, closing his eyes, content to lie at Hallie's bare feet, where he knew he would always be warm and welcome.

* * * * *

Celebrate 60 years of pure reading pleasure with Harlequin®!

Harlequin Presents® is proud to introduce its gripping new miniseries,
THE ROYAL HOUSE OF KAREDES.
An exquisite coronation diamond, split as a symbol of a warring royal family's feud, is missing! But whoever reunites the diamond halves will rule all....

Welcome to eight brand-new titles that unfold to reveal the stories of kings and queens, princes and princesses torn apart by pride and power, but finally reunited by love.

Step into the world of Karedes with
BILLIONAIRE PRINCE, PREGNANT MISTRESS
Available July 2009 from Harlequin Presents®.

ALEXANDROS KAREDES, SNOW DUSTING the shoulders of his leather jacket and glittering like jewels in his dark hair, stood at the door. Maria felt the blood drain from her head.

"Good evening, Ms. Santos."

His voice was as she remembered it. Deep. Husky. Perfect English, but with the faintest hint of a Greek accent. And cold, as cold as it had been that awful morning she would never forget, when he'd accused her of horrible things, called her terrible names....

"Aren't you going to ask me in?"

She fought for composure. Last time they'd

faced each other, they'd been on his turf. Now they were on hers. She was in command here, and that meant everything.

"There's a sign on the door downstairs," she said, her tone every bit as frigid as his. "It says, 'No soliciting or vagrants.'"

His lips drew back in a wolfish grin. "Very amusing."

"What do you want, Prince Alexandros?"

A tight smile eased across his mouth and it killed her that even now, knowing he was a vicious, arrogant man, she couldn't help but notice what a handsome mouth it was. Chiseled. Generous. Beautiful, like the rest of him, which made him living proof that beauty could, indeed, be only skin deep.

"Such formality, Maria. You were hardly so proper the last time we were together."

She knew his choice of words was deliberate. She felt her face heat; she couldn't help that but she damned well didn't have to let him lure her into a verbal sparring match.

"I'll ask you once more, your highness. What do you want?"

"Ask me in and I'll tell you."

"I have no intention of asking you in. Tell me

why you're here or don't. It's your choice, just as it will be my choice to shut the door in your face."

He laughed. It infuriated her but she could hardly blame him. He was tall—six two, six three—and though he stood with one shoulder leaning against the door frame, hands tucked casually into the pockets of the jacket, his pose was deceptive. He was strong, with the leanly muscled body of a well-trained athlete.

She remembered his body with painful clarity. The feel of him under her hands. The power of him moving over her. The taste of him on her tongue.

Suddenly, he straightened, his laughter gone. "I have not come this distance to stand in your doorway," he said coldly, "and I am not going to leave until I am ready to do so. I suggest you stand aside and stop behaving like a petulant child."

A petulant child? Was that what he thought? This man who had spent hours making love to her and had then accused her of—of trading her body for profit?

Except it had not been love, it had been sex. And the sooner she got rid of him, the better.

She let go of the doorknob and stepped aside. "You have five minutes."

He strolled past her, bringing cold air and the scent of the night with him. She swung toward him, arms folded. He reached past her, pushed the door closed, then folded his arms, too. She wanted to open the door again but she'd be damned if she was going to get into a who's-in-charge-here argument with him. She was in charge, and he would surely see a tussle over the ground rules as a sign of weakness.

Instead, she looked past him at the big clock above her worktable.

"Ten seconds gone," she said briskly. "You're wasting time, your highness."

"What I have to say will take longer than five minutes."

"Then you'll just have to learn to economize. More than five minutes, I'll call the police."

Instantly, his hand was wrapped around her wrist. He tugged her toward him, his dark-chocolate eyes almost black with anger.

"You do that and I'll tell every tabloid shark I can contact about how Maria Santos tried to buy a five-hundred-thousand-dollar commission by seducing a prince." He smiled thinly. "They'll lap it up."

* * * * *

What will it take for this billionaire prince to realize he's falling in love with his mistress...?
Look for
BILLIONAIRE PRINCE, PREGNANT MISTRESS
by Sandra Marton
Available July 2009 from Harlequin Presents®.

HARLEQUIN
60 YEARS
of pure reading pleasure

We'll be spotlighting a different series every month throughout 2009 to celebrate our 60th anniversary.

Look for Harlequin® Presents in July!

THE ROYAL HOUSE of KAREDES

TWO CROWNS, TWO ISLANDS, ONE LEGACY
A royal family, torn apart by pride and its lust for power, reunited by purity and passion

Step into the world of Karedes beginning this July with

BILLIONAIRE PRINCE, PREGNANT MISTRESS
by
Sandra Marton

Eight volumes to collect and treasure!

REQUEST YOUR FREE BOOKS!

2 FREE NOVELS PLUS 2 FREE GIFTS!

Silhouette

n o c t u r n e™

Dramatic and Sensual Tales of Paranormal Romance.

YES! Please send me 2 FREE Silhouette® Nocturne™ novels and my 2 FREE gifts (gifts are worth about $10). After receiving them, if I don't wish to receive any more books, I can return the shipping statement marked "cancel." If I don't cancel, I will receive 4 brand-new novels every other month and be billed just $4.47 per book in the U.S. or $4.99 per book in Canada. That's a savings of about 15% off the cover price! It's quite a bargain! Shipping and handling is just 25¢ per book*. I understand that accepting the 2 free books and gifts places me under no obligation to buy anything. I can always return a shipment and cancel at any time. Even if I never buy another book from Silhouette, the two free books and gifts are mine to keep forever.

238 SDN ELS4   338 SDN ELXG

Name	(PLEASE PRINT)	
Address		Apt. #
City	State/Prov.	Zip/Postal Code

Signature (if under 18, a parent or guardian must sign)

Mail to the **Silhouette Reader Service:**

IN U.S.A.: P.O. Box 1867, Buffalo, NY 14240-1867
IN CANADA: P.O. Box 609, Fort Erie, Ontario L2A 5X3

Not valid to current subscribers of Silhouette Nocturne books.

Want to try two free books from another line?
Call 1-800-873-8635 or visit www.morefreebooks.com.

* Terms and prices subject to change without notice. Prices do not include applicable taxes. Sales tax applicable in N.Y. Canadian residents will be charged applicable provincial taxes and GST. Offer not valid in Quebec. This offer is limited to one order per household. All orders subject to approval. Credit or debit balances in a customer's account(s) may be offset by any other outstanding balance owed by or to the customer. Please allow 4 to 6 weeks for delivery. Offer available while quantities last.

Your Privacy: Silhouette is committed to protecting your privacy. Our Privacy Policy is available online at www.eHarlequin.com or upon request from the Reader Service. From time to time we make our lists of customers available to reputable third parties who may have a product or service of interest to you. If you would prefer we not share your name and address, please check here. ☐

SN09

In 2009 Harlequin celebrates
60 years of pure reading pleasure!

We're marking this occasion by offering
16 **FREE** full books to download and read.

Visit

www.HarlequinCelebrates.com

to choose from a variety of
great romance stories
that are absolutely **FREE!**

(Total approximate retail value of $60)

We invite you to visit and share the Web site
with your friends, family
and anyone who enjoys reading.

Silhouette

nocturne™

COMING NEXT MONTH

Available July 4, 2009

#67 WILD WOLF • Karen Whiddon
The Pack

There's a new wolf in town, and it's up to Simon Caldwell
to assess the threat. To his shock, the female, Raven,
is young and undeniably attractive. When he is ordered
to exterminate her, Simon knows he must befriend and
protect her. But can a wild wolf be tamed by love?

#68 THE HIGHWAYMAN • Michele Hauf
Wicked Games

Feared in the paranormal realm, the Highwayman kills
demons as well as their conduits—familiars. But it is the
demon he harbors within his own soul that plagues him
the most. As a familiar, Aby Jones would normally be on
his hit list, but he suspects she may be his salvation in
more ways than one....